The Author

Best of Luck Kari + John
Bon Voyage
Susan

Books by Constance Beresford-Howe

CONSTANCE BERESFORD-HOWE

The Book of Eve

An M&S Paperback from
McClelland & Stewart Inc.
The Canadian Publishers

An M&S Paperback from McClelland & Stewart Inc.
First printing February 1989

Reprinted 1992

Canadian Cataloguing in Publication Data

Beresford-Howe, Constance, 1922–
The book of Eve

(M&S paperback)
ISBN 0-7710-1208-X

I. Title.
PS8503.E72B66 1989   C813'.54   C88-094983-X
PR9199.3.B47B66 1989

Cover illustration by Linda Montgomery
Cover design by David Wyman

Printed and bound in Canada by Webcom Limited

McClelland & Stewart Inc.
The Canadian Publishers
481 University Avenue
Toronto, Ontario
M5G 2E9

for Christopher

my dear Adam

The real surprise—to me anyway—was not really what I did, but how I felt afterwards. Shocked, of course. But not guilty. You might say, and be right, that the very least a woman can be is shocked when she walks out on a sick and blameless husband after forty years. But to feel no guilt at all—feel nothing, in fact, but simple relief and pleasure—that did seem odd, to say the least. How annoying for God (not to mention Adam), after all, if Eve had just walked out of Eden without waiting to be evicted, and left behind her pangs of guilt, as it were, with her leaf apron?

In any case, I just walked out. There was no quarrel with Burt. No crisis at all. The clock chimed nine-thirty. I laid down the breakfast tray carefully (an apple and a cup of cocoa) on the hall desk, and went to my room and packed. Not a word to anyone, even myself, by way of apology or excuse. Why? And why just then? Truly I'm not sure yet, although my name is Eva.

Our house was full of clocks rustling their self-importance and coughing delicately like people in church—they had something to do with it. So did my first old-age pension cheque, which had come the day before like a hint. But what chiefly stopped me was the cold white autumn light pouring through the landing window as I climbed up with the tray. It seemed to bleach the stairway into something like a high white cell. The night before on TV I'd seen cells like that in Viet Nam or somewhere, for political prisoners. You saw them crouched at the bottom of narrow cages, looking up at the light. I've never had a political conviction in my life, unless you count being bored by politics. But there I was just the same. Under bars.

Behind the bedroom door Burt gave his dry, irritable little cough. In a few minutes he would call me in a voice sharp and light with his morning pain. The cup of cocoa on the tray one minute steamed blandly and the next wobbled and slopped itself into the saucer. His mouth would press tight in disgust. "Can't you—" he would say, exasperated, "can't you—"

What I packed first (the whole thing took only ten minutes) was *Wuthering Heights* and a poetry anthology from my bedside shelf; but I didn't forget the grosser animal, and also took along my blood-pressure pills, glasses, hairbrush, and warm old-woman underpants. At the last minute I pulled out the plug of the little FM radio, Neil's birthday present, and tucked it under my arm.

And that was all. Out I went. There was a grey skin puckering on the cocoa as I passed it. On the stairs came his thin voice: "Eva!" I closed the front door on it.

No trouble finding a taxi on Monkland Avenue. Dry, grey October day, touch of frost. Nobody I recognized about. The only hard thing about the whole escape was getting all my possessions—radio, suitcase, and ample rump—crammed into the cab with any kind of dignity. The driver considerately pretended not to notice what a struggle this was. As soon as I got settled and found some breath, I paused to count my money. The pension cheque and fourteen eighty-nine in house money. Not much to kidnap yourself on, to be sure. But enough.

"Where to, lady?" the driver asked.

And of course it was then my legs began to shake.

The shaking moved up clear through me, belly and bones. For a minute I thought it might turn into crying or being sick; then with cold hands at my mouth I was astonished to find it was laughter in there, shaking to get out. The driver waited without interest, bored eyes on the traffic.

"Well, you tell me," I said, pressing a Kleenex against my sense of irony. He gave me a wary glance then, and I blew my nose to stop the laughing. Disgraceful. Shocking way to behave, all round. And where to, lady? Where, indeed? I had not given that a single thought. Certainly I couldn't go to Neil and his bitchy elegance of a wife. Or to our few friends who weren't dead or living in Arizona; they would be embarrassed, or scandalized, or both. No; I'd go it alone, and the farther away I could make it, the better. But of course you can't get far on a total of ninety-two eighty-nine, and my own bank account was down to nearly zero after a new winter coat. A bus to somewhere? Or a hotel here for a day or two, until I could get myself organized?

No, because getting organized in a place like the Laurentien Hotel, say, with its Murray's food and rules on every door would simply mean going back.

"No," I said out loud and put away the Kleenex. The driver waited resignedly. "Just drive downtown, will you?" The engine gnashed its teeth and we shot forward. "Right downtown—somewhere near St. Lawrence Main." Because now that I was collecting my wits a bit, I realized someone from Notre Dame de Grâce couldn't find a better place to hide than the other side of Montreal. I could find a room somewhere in the crowded French east end, and it would do perfectly. As for later on, and what to do then, I hadn't the least idea. I sat back on the cab's torn upholstery and we skimmed away through the neat, respectable rows of prosperous flats, full of decent women at their custodial jobs—wheeling babies, raking leaves, lugging bags of food. And I waited to feel guilty, properly horrified at what I was doing. Nothing at all stirred except a quite objective interest in what would happen next. Not to have the faintest idea what I might do—or become—was a peculiarly new and interesting experience, all by itself.

Of course it turned out that I'd forgotten all sorts of necessary things like toothpaste and extra shoes and my strong-willed girdle. Possibly I wasn't quite so cool and objective as I'd like to think. But I couldn't help admiring myself for doing anything so wicked. Not everyone could have done it, specially with my Anglican upbringing. How cross God must have been —if he kept track at all of such lapses as mine. And quite possibly he was the kind of person who did. Somebody like the chap that drove my taxi, with eyes like the dots on dice, disapproving of the whole cab-taking race, even though he couldn't exist without them.

No sleep at all last night, otherwise I'd never be speculating at this point on the nature of God. But it was far from unpleasant to lie awake thinking, even tingling with nervous fatigue, with my old friend the tension headache licking at my forehead, and counting over with real dismay how little was left of my cash. Because I felt excited as a girl, and happy enough to fly.

What a bit of luck to find this place, for one thing. Not more than two crow-miles from N.D.G., but a different world. You could immerse in it; become invisible. Rue de la Visitation, let me hide myself in thee.

In this district all the streets below Sherbrooke are narrow rows of senile, eccentric houses peering out of grimy dormer windows set high under fanciful mansard roofs. Iron lace and absurd crenellated towers crown them; they haven't been painted for at least a suitcase, and my pressure was up, everything throbbed. So I said, "I'll give you fifty a month for it."

"There's water-tax extra, a dollar fifty a month," Mrs. M. said at once. Of course she had no blood to have pressure with. And so we agreed, and the place was mine.

Long, suspicious negotiations then to cash my cheque and extort some change from it. Then a brief wrangle when I discovered the gas stove had only one functioning burner. But finally I was blissfully, blessedly alone. The place was my empire. The door was locked. I kicked off my shoes and lay right down in Blin & Blin on the degenerate sofa-bed and closed my eyes. Everything throbbed for a long time. And then I actually fell asleep.

And who would believe it possible to wake up in these circumstances as happy as a birthday child? I opened my eyes into a perfect, self-centered bliss without past or future, and rejoiced in everything I saw. Inspected every inch of my new place without a twinge of dismay, and then sat down to count my money—or what was left of it. Even this didn't depress me. Made a long shopping list and prepared to sally out to buy supplies. Shoes on again, climbed the basement stairs after a long grope for the light switch, and locked up my own door with my own key.

A cluttered little Chinese grocery-shop down the hill, full of colour and vegetable smells. A five-and-ten on Craig Street. A couple of hours later, home again, the door locked behind me, puffing, with two huge paper bags to unpack. Happy. I had bought two strong light-bulbs, cleaning powder (the MacNab influence, no doubt), toilet paper, a saucepan, a set of Japanese cutlery, a can-opener, a plate and mug, a facecloth and towel, matches for the stove, staples like salt, sugar, tea, and tins of soup, a few fresh things like butter and eggs, milk, and bread. A postcard and

13

stamp to inform the Prime Minister where to send my next pension cheque. It all tore an amazing hole in my money. I didn't care. I'd even bought a bottle of cheap sherry—a piece of wicked extravagance and folly. Two ninety left. But that didn't really worry me. Nothing did. I found a corkscrew and a bread knife in the kitchen drawer and a frypan and scrubbing-brush under the sink. Rapturous as a kid playing house. Sun grinned in at the dirty window overhead. Two blankets revealed themselves when I opened the sofa-bed; under the chair-cushion I found a quarter, a copy of *Playboy*, and a ballpoint pen. Across the hall the furnace grumbled peacefully like a snoring monster. Not another sound except the distant scurry of MacNab, a muttering TV, once a child's wail, a dog's bark, a door-bang. All remote as sounds on another planet. Deeply satisfying.

I set up my books on an end-table, plugged in my radio, and switched it on. Mozart obliged. I found an old peanut-butter jar and drank rather a lot of sherry out of it. When dusk painted the windows an opaque blue I heated soup and ate it, then scrubbed out the bath, filled it up, and had a long, contented soak with *Playboy*. After that I brushed my teeth and climbed into bed. Clean, happy, and innocent as a lamb. For a few hours I slept fathoms deep in the dark, without a dream.

And then I woke up to hear my heart beating. I began then to count and think. Great mistakes, both.

The trouble is, you never can escape a righteous upbringing. Right now I was a success—an escaped prisoner never likely to be recaptured. What's more, I hadn't the slightest urge to explain or apologize to Burt or Neil. And yet, I wanted to justify my ways to somebody—God, perhaps—because, come to think of it, nobody else really knew me. A bit of cheek, perhaps, to address Him person-to-person; if only I could write Him a letter.

Reverend Sir:

I realize I owe You some kind of explanation for yesterday, during which I broke quite a few of Your ten rules (though I've often wondered whether Moses didn't forge some of them).

You see, I'd like to make it clear that I ran away not just from the servitude of nursing Burt, running the house, shopping and cleaning up, and all that drab routine. Nor from the confinement, even, though that was bad. As You know, he was haunted by the fear of fire, and hated being left alone in the house even for short intervals while I did necessary errands in the neighbourhood. He couldn't get out in the winter months himself at all, and of course it was hard for him, caged up inside his pain, to keep a sense of proportion. But one of my few pleasures, especially in the years after Neil's marriage, was browsing through antique shops, where I discovered treasures like my spinet desk, a Lismer drawing, and a Belleek tea-set—all such bargains even Burt couldn't complain much. But in the last few years, he made such a misery every time I wanted to go out for a few hours on these hunts that finally I had to give them up altogether. And because that one little private pleasure was cut off, I festered with resentment. Inwardly only—though I don't claim that as a virtue; I couldn't face quarrelling.

"Burt, someone can come in and sit with you for a few hours—Janet next door has offered to, more than once."

"I don't want to be under an obligation to the neighbours."

"Well, then, why can't we pay someone to—"

"You want a stranger in here?—"

You see. It was no use reasoning with him. No

15

use exploding in anger, either. So I said nothing; just festered. And took to eating for consolation and pleasure. Gradually I swelled with fat, loose, heavy flesh like another prison I still lug around. The doctor warned me, and prescribed pills for hypertension; it was no use. I went on eating and eating—during the day, like an addict, I bridged meals with chocolates; I ate hot rolls with butter and jam, slices of pie with whipped cream; at night I took butter tarts or a wedge of iced cake to eat in bed with a book.

After a while I came to feel as if all this fat were a sort of disguise. No one knew me. Burt, who saw me every day, least of all. Neil, who rarely saw me, had cares of his own, including four children, so he had to avoid recognizing what he knew of me. And there was no one else.

Do You realize, I wonder, what submerged identities women like me can have? How repressed and suppressed we are by a life that can give us no kind of self-expression? Unless You really are female after all, as the Women's Lib girls insist, even You can't know what it's like to be invisible for years on end. To live locked up. Never spontaneous. Never independent. Never free, even to use those four-letter words we all know, because the chief duty of females, we were taught, was to practise the restraints of civilization, not explore its possibilities.

So my solitary confinement has been pretty hard to distinguish from death itself. Oh, hell— if You'll pardon the expression—that sounds emotional and exaggerated, but You know what I mean. God, I hate whiners, and even to You I won't snivel with self-pity.

It would have been different if my life before Burt got arthritis had been full of colour and interest and the richness of love and loving. But if You don't mind my saying so, I got a damn small share of those things, so small that coming up to my seventieth year I couldn't help feeling both cheated and panicky.

Well, that's my case. Does it make any sense to You? I hope so, because, Sir, I'd like You to respect me, even if You disapprove. And I'd be glad if You could give a bit of advice on what to do with my freedom, now I've stolen it. Hoping to hear from You in the near future,

> I remain,
> Yours disobediently,
> Eva.

Which would be all very well if God ever answered His mail.

Naturally it was raining by the time light came. My headache had bloomed into a fine specimen and my back-muscles gave a thin scream every time I moved. Not moving at all would have been easy, but lying still encouraged the old thinking and counting, and built up much depression. Now those indignant self-reproaches I thought I'd escaped saw their chance to come around and put their tongues out at me. Worst of all was the nagging voice of common sense, asking things like How could you leave, if not home, all that good walnut and mahogany furniture, specially the corner cabinet and the spinet desk so lovingly restored . . . the Lawren Harris, the Lismer drawing, the sterling flatware, even the worn Oriental rugs that still glowed—how could you leave all that, not to mention your status as respectable wife, mother, and grandmother? Even your identity you've left behind like rubbish. Surely you must have had some kind of brainstorm.

Lying there, feet cold, I thought, "It's true. Go home, you crazy old cow. Tell everybody you're sorry. This is impossible. What do you think you're doing in this awful basement?"

And of course I could then hear Burt's pedantic

voice adding the accountant's viewpoint. "Just how do you propose to live on seventy-eight dollars a month? Because you can hardly expect me to contribute, can you, to a wife who just walks off like that, without a word? Sulking, I suppose, because I won't sell this house and move into some cardboard apartment at a ridiculous rent. You've always been secretive. And foolish with money. Hold on here and this place will double in value the next ten years. And of course by Quebec law I'm not bound to support you unless you live under my roof. Well, you can't live on the pension cheque, and at your age you can hardly expect to get a job. All your life you've been spoiled, protected. Live on seventy-eight a month! What about shoes and drugs and dentists? Some people might manage it, perhaps, but not you."

Meekly I conceded the perfect truth of all this. Furthermore, I could admit now that this place was more humble than home. Last night (though I'd pretended not to) I distinctly saw a bug slide away down the sink-drain. Rain had leaked in for years at the window over my head, leaving a long rusty stain on the wall. The air smelled of dust and tomcats and furnace oil. By daylight the room, with its battered old furniture, looked sordid as a waiting-room in hell. It might be possible to fix the place up—if you had a few thousand dollars—but my bank account contained exactly thirty-nine dollars. I hadn't even had the wits to bring along my few pieces of jewellery to sell. (But maybe Burt would send them along . . . they were my own. And some of my shoes. . . .)

It was only seven o'clock, but I got up and began to dress, very slowly because of the headache and the stiff back, both of which instantly got worse. It would take only a few minutes to pack up and phone home. He would be sour and vindictive, but what was new about that? I'd accepted it for over forty years.

"No, Burt, I never really liked you," a surprised, rude little voice said inside me. "I married you because
18

I wanted to be married and I wanted children. The ring, the bed, the security. But you I never really liked. And I suspect the same may be true on your side. It's just habit or inertia or cowardice that's kept us together all this time." I groped for a chair to put on my stockings, and depression like a lead weight seemed to push me into it. "And yet he's always been what people call a good husband, a good provider. Perfectly faithful. Right, always, about everything concrete and unimportant. Thrifty. Decent. Not ungenerous in some ways. In fact now, he might . . . he just might . . . if only he'd send me the diamond rings, even, that were Gran's. They might bring as much as five hundred . . . they're mine, after all, he can't keep them, can he?"

"Of course he can. He can do anything he likes."

And so could I.

With that, my headache vanished, as if turned off by a switch. I stood up stiffly and finished dressing. Tomorrow, or whenever the rain stopped, I would take the bus and go to the bank. Bug-killer and putty and a broom wouldn't cost a fortune. Nor would a phone call. Not to Burt. I still had the sore back, and the very thought of a little chat with Burt was enough to start the headache on the road back. But I would ring Neil right away. Poor boy. A pity to drag him into this, but I had no choice. He might be able to get more out of his father than I could. It was worth trying. At the very least, I had to let them both know I was all right.

"Neil?" (At the office, not at home, in case Elegance should frown.)

"Mother, for God's sake, is it you? Where are you?"

"Now just a minute—"

"Just a minute, Mum—Sheila, I don't want to be disturbed—just ask Kalmer to wait—now, Mum. Are you all right?"

19

Dear Neil, voice gentle under the hectoring edge of worry. It was really a pity I had to do this to him.

"I'm fine, dear. Sorry if you worried. But Neil, I want to ask you—"

"Mother, I've been worried sick. Where the hell are you? I called everybody I could think of last night, nobody knew a thing, and I couldn't bring myself to go to the police. And as for Dad, he's fit to be tied."

Rather shamefaced grin. "I'll bet he is."

"But where *are* you? Was there some kind of row? What made you just take off like that, without a word to anybody?"

"I don't know, really. Neil, what I want to ask you is—"

"Well, of course I know things have never been exactly idyllic with you and Dad, but I never thought —I mean after all these years—"

"That's it, maybe, dear. All those years."

"But Mum, he's really upset. I don't think you—I've never seen him like this. Of course he's started a bad attack; I had to get a nurse in this morning. But the thing is, whatever's wrong can surely be put right. He cares a lot about you, you must know that."

Meant to keep this conversation strictly matter-of-fact, but perspiring now under the arms like a surgeon with his first patient on the table.

"Neil, I don't want to go into all that. There's no point really. All I want to say is, I don't intend to go back. What I called for was to let you know I'm all right, not dead yet or anything. And to ask if you'd please get me some of my things from the house."

"Some of your things! But Mum—"

"Yes, my shoes, for instance—"

"But Mum—"

"Dear, I do wish you wouldn't keep on quacking 'But Mum'. Your father will get on quite well with a practical nurse or a housekeeper. The price will half kill him, but I can't help that. I am not going back. That's quite final. But I need some of my things

20

rather badly, like my extra shoes, and if you could also get hold of my bits of jewellery—"

"Mother, listen, you'll feel completely different in a day or two, I know you will. Dad's irritable, he says sharp things; but you know perfectly well he . . . of course what you need is a little change and rest. He knows that as well as I do. Why don't you go off to New York for a week or so and see some bright lights? Or have a little whirl in Florida? You haven't had a holiday in years, really. I'd be glad to provide the—"

"No. I mean, no thanks." Why is it, I wondered crossly, that truly good people like my son seem able to speak only in clichés.

"But Mum—"

Sigh. "Neil, all I want is my shoes."

"But Mother, you can't just—look here, where are you? I'll come along and pick you up for lunch and we can—"

"No. Thanks, dear, but no."

A baffled pause at the other end. Mustering of forces mutually.

"Whether you like it or not, Mum, I'll have to see you, we've got to discuss this thing. Why won't you tell me where you are? It isn't reasonable—you've got to—"

"No, it isn't reasonable. I'm sorry, Neil."

"Wait a second—don't ring off for God's sake. Look, how are you off for money?"

"Oh, I have a bit tucked away in the bank. Enough for a while." That sounded grand; quite airy and confident.

"For a while. But then what? All you've got of your own is the pension. And you can't possibly live on that. And then how is Dad going to manage without you? How can you have the heart—"

There are times when I remember that Neil is Burt's son, all right.

"Are we talking about hearts or cash here? If it's money, I was hoping you might persuade your father to give me a little every month. But if he won't, I'll find some way to manage. I am not going back to him, for that or any other reason."

Another pause.

"Of course I'll speak to Dad about it. But he's not very likely to—"

"No, I know. Well, I have no resources to go after a legal separation or anything like that; but I did think we might between us settle what's fair. For the last eighteen years, after all, with that arthritis of his, I've waited on the man hand and foot and got nothing much more for it than my room and board. But I simply won't whine to you . . . forget all that. Only perhaps you could discuss it with him, a small allowance. Even fifty dollars a month would make all the difference. But make no mistake about it, I won't go back."

Long speech. Heart banging unpleasantly. Silence at the other end. My poor Neil. Peace-maker, always defeated, like all the gentle compromisers.

"And if you could just pack up the rest of my clothes and things, and the little velvet jewel box in my top drawer. . . ."

"But Mum—" One last feeble quack.

"I'll call you again—say on Friday." (That would give Burt time for two tantrums and a recovery—perhaps.)

"That's nearly a week—"

"Yes."

"Look, Mum, can you manage all right? Let me give you some cash at least, to have by you. And for God's sake tell me where you're staying."

"No, I'm perfectly all right for money, and it's better this way. Just have a talk with your father and I'll call you Friday."

But peace-makers have their own weapons. Before I could hang up, he said, "Mum, I want you to know how much this is hurting him, his pride—and it's a worry for me too, if that matters. And Kim has been really upset."

22

Not fair, not fair. Lovely Kim at fourteen with her long nut-brown hair and shy eyes (and silly dog's name, the mother's trendy choice, of course)—a low blow to bring my Kim into this and make tremors start climbing up my legs again. Would she think of me with scorn now I've become a sort of geriatric hippie?

"I'll call Friday," I said quickly and hung up.

For a minute I stayed in the stuffy phone booth, just breathing in and out and staring down at my rain-stained shoes. Then I tugged the door open and trudged slowly up the street, back to my hole. Rain the whole way. But as I unlocked Mrs. MacNab's door I thought, Well, he did leave one out; that's something—"You'll Live to Regret This." For some reason that cheered me up a bit.

It rained with such religious fervour all week that it wasn't till Friday that I went along to the bank to close my account. A nervous business, going along that familiar street, dreading an encounter with neighbours. Luckily I saw no one I knew in the bank and, hurrying to the bus-stop with my coat-collar well turned up, thought I'd made a clean getaway. But ahead of me in a cluster of people at the traffic light, I caught sight of tall, thin-as-a-pole Janet Gordon from next door, and my heart immediately jumped into the top of my mouth.

At once I began to sidle out of the group, but she never glanced back my way, being absorbed in chat with a friend. And I paused in my flight, because what I could hear of the chat turned out, entertainingly, to be about me.

"—after all those years—more devoted husband never lived—of course you know I always—something odd—never would join any clubs or groups—once told me she'd rather be grilled alive than play bridge. Frivolous. But I do feel sorry for him, poor soul."

"Where did she go?"

"Florida. Took all his bonds with her."

"How awful," said the friend sincerely.

The light changed and I dropped farther behind, trying to rearrange my face, which had already attracted the attention of two cheeky little boys. In Florida! Who would ever have credited Janet with so much creative imagination! And that touch about the bonds was perfect. So much more impressive and believable than the truth, as art should always be. And who knows—maybe a wish-fulfilment of Janet's own. Her husband had a model railway in the basement and false teeth that clicked.

Much diverted as long as these reflections lasted. Soon I climbed aboard an eastbound bus and relaxed, settling down for the long ride with the content of one who has avoided unpleasantness successfully, without at all deserving to.

The days became long, then, and the nights longer.

Having no one to talk to was the biggest change. Communication between me and Burt of course used to take place at the lowest level of exchange—we traded in nothing but the smallest of talk, expertly maneuvering, always, to avoid a row. "Colder today." "Too much salt in this. Can't you—" "We need potatoes." "The paper boy's late." Hardly stimulating dialogue. But not to speak out loud a single word, for two days at a time, as I've more than once done since the move—a very odd feeling grew, as if I were isolated on some forgotten island, or walking mute through someone else's dream. There were times when I wondered if I were real.

I hardly ever saw the other occupants of the Mac-Nab house. Most of them no doubt went dutifully off to jobs every morning, while I sat up reading or scribbling or thinking most of the night, and slept all morning. There was an ancient couple in the front rooms; they inched out cautiously in the noon sun, tall her holding short him gingerly by the arm, both old parchment faces set with effort. They never spoke, though he always lifted a tremulous hand to his hat. Another old gaffer in a belted overcoat to his heels often hurried in and out talking to himself in some impenetrable foreign language. A harried young mother came and went, too, hauling along two grimy toddlers; but she had nothing to say that wasn't said better by her look of controlled desperation. She never said a word to the kids either, except by way of a jerk or push. Somewhere up on the top floor lived a couple of smart-jacketed queers, but they spoke only to each other and to their prancing poodle.

Only Mrs. MacNab, surprisingly, turned out to be a compulsive talker, though she had just two topics. One was her son, Findlay, an old young man who seemed to spend most of his life putting out garbage. The other was their joint struggle with all the problems and hardships of running the house, keeping it clean, paying the taxes, collecting the rents, and so on and on and on. Soon I learned to time my entrances and exits to those intervals when she was emptying suds. Better silence than some kinds of conversation. But it all made for a lot of introspection; and being so totally alone with myself was not always comfortable.

Thinking about abstract things is something no woman willingly does, and I had no intention of beginning now. But somehow all kinds of speculations drifted along in my solitude, specially after dark. I was no nearer after a week than I'd been at the beginning to understanding exactly what made me walk out of my snug middle-class security into this place. But I did a lot of rather vague and muddled thinking about my life generally, trying to see if it made any kind of pattern or sense. Very hard to find much of either.

This century and I are about the same age, so it would be easy, even if not really true, to say I'm a typical twentieth-century product of desiccated moral codes. Or a victim of its two diseases, comfort and boredom. But it's so unflattering to be a product or a victim. No, if I'm a product at all it's of the nineteenth century, which in many ways hasn't ended yet. Brought up to believe in the Christian ethos, vaguely accept its preposterous claim, and at the same time, with no strong sense of irony, live by the Victorian motto—Possess, or Prosper, or something like that. Certainly I lived by that contradictory code, going to church, teaching school, marrying Burt; yes, it divided me even in the midst of all that business I thought of as love with Pat. If I had a coherent motive through it all, it was acquisitive: collect, invest, and then count the interest, as if some time or other *the* thing of value would come along, and I could then buy it.

And then, without warning, I walked out. (And have been feverishly counting over your money ever since, you old fool.) Since then I've been sitting in parks with the bowing pigeons. Or walking around the streets looking in the windows of pawnshops and second-hand clothing stores and Chinese restaurants. Perfectly idle and pointless days. I eat hunched over a book at the kitchen table, careless of crumbs, belches, or noisy chewings. My hair needs doing and funds are too low for that. Have to renew the pressure pills, which leaves so little of my dwindling cash that I don't dare buy so much as a toothpick. My shoes finally dried out after their second drenching (the damn rain never stopped all week), but they're stiff and shrivelled now, hurt my corns a lot, and interfere plenty with philosophical reflection. All I know for sure is that being alone like this, holed up in a dusty basement, is something of value, and I'll never go back.

A crazy conclusion, I suppose. Cruel, too. All Burt's pains, of mind and body and spirit, are absolutely real and sharp. And there's Neil, who never asked to be born to us, or to be the only one between parents like millstones. No, there is no health in me, in the prayer-book sense. When Neil finally corners me into a meeting, I'll have no defence at all; I know beforehand he's right about everything. Once I was as sure as maybe he still is that kindness is the supreme virtue. Now I know it's no such thing. Don't ask me what is, honesty maybe. But who am I to preach anything but sedition. Because nowadays I think much more highly of sloth, greed, pride, avarice, anger, etc., than I used to do.

No defence for me at all. No right to expect even justice, much less mercy, from God or man (i.e., my son). Then why do I swim across a good part of each dark, insomniac night worrying how to manage the problem of my water-warped shoes, so Neil won't notice them when we meet, or my hair with the perm all grown out. It seems so important to look respectable; and if it really is important, then I have no business here. None whatever.

Quite often I got up in the dark, fumbled on a light, and gave myself a big dose of cheap sherry. It's good against logic.

Finally what I did was buy some of those plastic rollers, and washed and set my own hair. It looked bad, but not as bad as before. And explored Dupuis's basement for cheap shoes, where I found some black pumps on a bargain table near my size. (Well, you don't find quadruple A's on sale often, life isn't that kind.) They went on, and I could walk in them, and they were only six dollars. Plus tax. Legs and feet still very good, slim and young. When I look down, can forget the fat old woman on top, so shoes are important twice over.

Of course Neil noticed absolutely nothing. After the first harried, curious glance, he avoided looking at me altogether. Which was really what I'd hoped for when I chose the place for us to meet. People who are lunching at the Ritz don't look at each other. It isn't

27

done. Any more than they really eat there, just peck, preen, and bow like the park pigeons. I noticed this for the first time, really, because for ten or fifteen minutes I chewed up my steak with so much enthusiasm (meat-hungry after a week of cheap food) that Neil ran out of small talk and began to look embarrassed, like a man having lunch with a tiger. Not comfortable to have lunch at the Ritz with a tiger, specially if you're related to it.

Probably that's why he so soon began to take a rather tough line with me, which is unlike him, and rather upset me, because it wasn't what I'd expected.

"Now, Mother," he began, as soon as my rudely polished plate had been taken away, "let's get down to it. I've had two or three talks with Dad about the whole thing, and there's no doubt that he's . . . very badly upset."

"You mean he's being intensely disagreeable."

Neil flushed. He never has gotten along well with his father, and characteristically blames himself for this.

"I mean he feels this more than you realize. You *know* him, after all—he never can, somehow, admit he's wrong about anything, even when he knows it. He just can't get the words out. But he looks terrible, Mum—old and pathetic. He knows he's been a burden. But honestly, I don't know how you could do it to him, when he needs you so much. And not to know even where you can be reached—"

There was no answer to this, which gave Neil confidence.

"Now I did get him to say this much—and from him it's a lot—that nothing whatever will be said when you come back. Not a word. You can see what he's trying to get across, can't you? For God's sake, you've lived with him forty years."

No answer to this, either. All true.

"Now what I suggest is this, Mum. You go on down to New York or Atlantic City for a bit of sun, and have

28

a little holiday. You need a change and rest. A couple of weeks and you won't know yourself. Dad said last night he'd pay the shot."

Triumphant, having played his high card, Neil sat back and lit his pipe. But when I still said nothing, just sat there looking down at my hands (still narrow and elegant like my feet, and a comfort to me), he appeared to think he might have been almost too persuasive, and to forestall tears patted my arm. In a hurry he went on, "No trouble getting you a plane reservation this very afternoon—what do you say?— and maybe you'd like to buy yourself a few clothes down there. You could do with some pretty things for a change. I've got a little present for you to spend."

That nearly did it. My dear son, my Neil and his kind heart with its rare flashes of insight and clumsy tact. He was the enemy, not Burt; with his sweetness and reason he was the real threat. All his life I'd fought against loving Neil too much, and that was all that helped me now.

"No, dear. I'm not going to New York. Or to Florida. Or back to your father. So if that's all you can suggest, we might as well let you get back to the office."

Carefully he laid his pipe on its side in the inadequate hotel ashtray. He looked older by some shift of expression or light; the stigmata of worn and worried middle age were clear on his fresh and pleasant face. Well, Neil was thirty-eight.

"Mum, you can't be serious. I mean, how can you manage—let's face the plain fact, you can't live on that pension."

"Your father won't make me an allowance, then."

"Well, I don't think he—I mean, when I first made the suggestion, he hit the roof, Mum, so I didn't bring it up again."

"All right, then. That's his privilege."

"But you simply can't live on—"

"Don't you worry about it, Neil. I'll manage."

"How can you say don't worry!" His blue eyes stared

at me in real anger. "When you won't even tell me where you're living—or how. Don't worry! You damned well can't live on air. And if Dad won't help, and you persist in living apart, I'll simply have to make up the difference myself. And I'd do it willingly enough if I weren't half out of my mind as it is, with every one of my kids in expensive damned schools and orthodontic braces. And that's the truth."

Felt terribly tired now. No emotions left, just tired out. Wanted to get away.

"I know how it is and I wouldn't take a penny from you, Neil; you know that."

He frowned at the water in his glass and then drank it off like hemlock. "It's a pity you took your School Board pension in a cash lump, you know; after fifteen years it would have brought you in something useful. . . ."

"Well, most of it went into a down payment on that house in N.D.G., which makes it half mine, surely. Has he thought of that, I wonder? You might mention it, perhaps, if the opportunity ever comes up."

"Yes, but you see the house is in his name; you never had a marriage contract, so you can't legally claim any part of the house as yours."

"Oh, I know all that."

Perhaps he was tired too, rubbing across his eyes like a child at bedtime. We sat there a minute without saying anything more. Then he made a big mistake.

"Of course I've talked this whole thing over with Rosemary, and she thinks—"

"My dear, I don't give a God-damn what Rosemary thinks."

Offended, he jerked back his head as if I'd bitten him. Caesar's wife, after all. The elegant product of Montreal's Square Mile, to be dismissed so rudely. I had always been scrupulously polite to and about Neil's wife—another of my many repressions—so to hear the truth now really shocked him.

"I know you mean well, dear, but it's no use. We

might as well go. I'm not going to change my mind, you know. Perhaps I'll get in touch with you again in a week or so. You're not to worry in the meantime, though—I'm perfectly well, I've found a cheap, comfortable place to live, and I am going to be all right. No need to fuss yourself or nag your father. After all, At My Age—" and to the surprise of both of us a big laugh broke out, jerking a few heads around—"well, you can see for yourself I'm perfectly all right."

But his reluctant smile showed just how dubious he was, suddenly, about that. When we said good-bye a few minutes later, his tone was indulgent as if he were humouring someone ill, and doing it with an effort, to conceal fear. He put me solicitously into a cab, after pushing a ten-dollar bill into my hand. And what a relief to sit down, the new shoes were torture.

"Now you be sure to call me, Mum, before the end of the week. Promise, now. I'll be seeing Dad before that, of course. Now take care of yourself. Sure you have—all you need?"

Couldn't get away fast enough from the anxiety in those mild eyes that so clearly said "She's a little— could she be getting a bit—? And if so, what do I do now?"

So the whole meeting shook me up, no denying. Worse than I expected it to, and in different places. When I got home (believe it or not, nervously checking to be sure he wasn't following me), and had the door safely locked, I flopped on the bed and tried to relax my arteries. Not much luck.

That night was bad. Dreams of my father in a wheelchair, crying because I wouldn't let him stand up. Calling and calling to me. Had to read a long time to shake it off. And all the next day Neil's words smarted like a spanking.

The morning after, though, I felt better and it occurred to me what a good idea it would be to give

31

the apartment a thorough housecleaning. It would look a hundred times better for a real scrub, wax, furniture polish, the whole bit. I'd borrow Mrs. M's vacuum cleaner, wash and starch the sad old curtains, maybe even buy a cheap remnant to cover the chair-cushion. Nobody needed to feel sorry for me. Nobody needed to imply I'd gone around some kind of senile bend. This place could be made to look quite decent, not a hole I was ashamed to let Neil see.

Astonishing how much energy this gave me, and how much I enjoyed planning the campaign. I trotted straight off to buy a bagful of cleaning things with the change from Neil's ten. Cheerfully I lugged it all home, and then lumbered upstairs again to borrow the vacuum. I worked all afternoon and late into the evening. A bit of shine, a smell of lemon oil, it was surprising what a difference they made to the place. I kept on working long after my back started to ache, and when at last I couldn't go on another minute, poured sherry, plopped into a chair, and felt as pleased as if I'd been forgiven.

MacNab syndrome next day, though. Woke early, heart in a great hurry, nausea, funny floating sensation in the legs. Damn fool, I thought, you've spot-removed yourself. It was really bad. Frightening, because the malaise was so general you couldn't nail it down to any one place or cause. So weak and queer generally I was afraid to try getting up. Watched the sun move on the wall and kept drifting near sleep; but a busy whispering somewhere in the arteries made me afraid to sleep in case it might be permanent. That left me alone with *timor mortis*, never a welcome guest. Met only once or twice before, and didn't like it then either.

Healthy as a trout all my life—never knew what pain was, even, till Neil was born. And even then, what I hated most was the feeling that in so impor-

tant a business as giving birth I had actually so little
to contribute. The pains began when they decided to
(in the middle of a Mary Pickford movie), they ac-
celerated and intensified at their own pace, and mus-
cles pushed the child out into the world without
consulting him at all, or me much. Like his concep-
tion, all (or nearly all) decided by and controlled by
some process outside the will; and I resented that,
because aren't we entitled, after all this business of
evolution, to a share of the responsibility? Lying there,
rhythmically assaulted by pain, I felt like a means to
an end, while the doctor, cheerfully lighting a cigarette, gossiped to Burt about the stock market. Of
course, eventually I was only too pleased to be chloro-
formed right out of the whole thing. But I resented
even more having no vote in the matter a couple of
years later when I miscarried, and with blood and tears
life was taken away instead of given. (Maybe Burt
had some queer feeling of his own about that—Doctor
Baird told me afterward that he'd asked to see the
fetus and wept over it. And Burt was a man so
squeamish he couldn't bear to dig a splinter out of
his own finger: odd of him to ask; odder, even, to
show so much feeling. Never really understood him.)

Understood him well enough, though, that time I
had the appendix out, recuperating at home, still in
bed, May visiting—he never liked her, I think her
crazy sense of humour made him nervous; there was
strain whenever she came. We were just talking casually when the subject of Burt came up, and May remarked mildly that he had a rather difficult tempera-
ment. God knows, not an overstatement. And I said
he'd never learned to develop some of his emotions or
control others—something like that—which, of course,
made him difficult to live with even to himself. Well,
he overheard it somehow, not above listening at doors.
And exploded in a violent tantrum, yelling loud
enough to terrify Neil, accusing me furiously of dis-
loyalty, among many other crimes. My temperature

33

went up that night, the incision stopped healing. It was the first time I realized just what I'd done to both of us by marrying him. I couldn't stop crying. Burt didn't speak to me for two weeks. My first lesson in psychosomatic medicine.

Well, poor old Burt, that long martyrdom of his to arthritis may have been his introduction. It must have illustrated the truth to him too, a thousand times over, in all those years of pain and crippling, of what our own inner diseases do to the flesh. But if he knew, he never said. Only became more acidulous, critical, touchy, narrow, cantankerous, exacting, fastidious, and bloody-minded than ever, as if determined to stay himself—and more so—in spite of it all.

The sun crept slowly along one wall, moved diagonally across a corner of the ceiling, and slid away. I grew thirsty. My feet ached with cold. But trying to sit up made me so dizzy I lay down again in a bit of a panic. I even thought of banging on the wall or shouting for help; but something prevented me. Some of Burt's stubborn pride, maybe. Besides, who would hear me, or answer if they did? I couldn't remember even the face, much less the identity, of a single tenant in the house.

By dusk I was drifting in a not-unpleasant state of indifference. After all, maybe this was the best way. Who needed or cared about me now? What was I, fat old parasite, member of the third sex now, an irrelevant and uncalled-for detail of the human race. And a swift exit had at least some dignity, unlike those horrible lingerings to be seen in nursing homes, where death is the friend who too seldom drops in. No, much better to accept it now, and go.

But of course I should have remembered what I'd learned at Neil's birth: executive decisions are made at headquarters. We aren't asked even for an opinion. As it grew dark, thirst began to torment me. At last, by laborious, dizzy stages, I managed to drag my trembling old carcass out of bed, across the room, out into the hall where the furnace rumbled indifferently. Clinging to the bathroom sink and gasping, ran water and drank. After a dubious minute, kept it down. Made my way back, shuffling and slow, but feeling a bit stronger and full of triumph.

Still in limbo all the next day. Rain rustling on the high windows, blearing the light. Dozed a lot, no real frontier between sleeping and waking, no discomfort but the cold feet. Early in the morning urgently needed to pee, and made it again to the bathroom, but felt sick and faint on the way, and took a long time to struggle back. In bed, finally, so exhausted and indifferent I really thought, So this is how it is. But nothing else except confused and disintegrating thoughts and the faint rustle of time pacing away.

It wasn't till night stood there black as a bat's ear that things began to clear a bit. Blundered to find the lamp switch. Then (very cautiously, not to offend any power that might be in charge) dragged a few steps to the chair where my coat hung, and hauled it back to bed to cover my legs. After a bit, a pleasant warmth. Head a bit clearer. Felt terribly empty. Some hot soup; phone room service. After another bit, realized another rugged safari to the kitchen would have to happen. Pulled the coat on (poor old Blin & Blin) and actually managed to dump left-over soup into a pot, heat it, and sit up at the crooked kitchen table to eat. Shaking the whole time like a wet dog, but still. Body woke up at last. Back in bed very coherent and alert, even though my legs still felt a bit disassociated and queer.

Well, one thing was plain enough by now. Living alone—or dying alone—like a rat in a cellar made all the rest a bad joke. I mean all that earnest confidence, all that effort. Sunday School, writing lessons with copybook maxims in pretty, fluent letters: A Man Is The Sum of His Achievements; a Master's diploma with its red seal ("Very nice, dear, even if a girl doesn't really need that sort of thing"—1922); piles of high-school essays hen-tracked with red-ink corrections; long strings of baby wash, rows of currant-jelly jars; more essays; "Cleopatra died from the bite of an aspirin"; ironing fourteen shirts a week; courses at night, fighting sleep in dusty lecture rooms ("What the hell do you want a Ph.D for? These days they're sweeping the streets for a meal."): Saving money. Saving fat and paper and bottles, making bandages, praying on my knees it would be over before Neil . . . carrying trays, massaging the thin, knotted shoulders, measuring out medicine, hurrying to the bank, the drug store, the grocery, the bank, home, the fruit shop, the cleaner's ("What the hell took you so long? I suppose you realize if ever there were a fire here . . ."). All that for this? Crazy. One or the other was. If nothing else, somebody to look after me could be the sum of my achievements. It made no sense at all to die down here with nobody to bring me a drink of water, after all that invested effort.

Slept quite a while, worn out by these conclusions.

Morning bright. Blaze of blue sky. Wind making the sun flash on the wall. Crawled to the kitchen, a bit steadier, drank tea. Thought, Where did I put the suitcase? No hurry. Maybe this afternoon be able to get dressed and pack up. Drain of sherry left in the bottle, laced the next cup with it. Idly contemplated the clean kitchen linoleum (blue and white squares excavated under all that grime), clear window full of light (a plant would thrive there now), sink scrubbed free of rust and purged of bugs—wait—wasn't that—ugh, yes, by God. Not quite purged. Ugly brute. Cheek of it. Delicate legs progressing, leisurely exploration. Even a pause while it seemed to glance up at the sun. Sluice it down the drain, But, hand on tap, didn't. Back glossy, taper shape functional, elegant, movement tentative—perceived me, was afraid, perhaps? After all, what harm was a bug or two going to do anybody? Wasn't there room enough in the world for both of us? He had as much right to live as I did, surely. More sense, if anything. Didn't ask a lot of damn-fool questions. Just lived. Just lived.

Stronger the next day, though still a bit shaky in the knees. Of course I didn't even look for the suitcase. Instead I spent hours in bed resting and thinking, while the whole day's light wheeled by. Perhaps because death had receded, I got to thinking about love. And of course sex. Me, that is, and love and sex, and Patrick. There seemed to be time to remember it all, at last. All the time in the world.

Properly organized, my affair with Pat should have begun with that throb of grand passion indicated in the movies by swelling music ("Rosalie, I Love You"), and ended with a bang of noble renunciation. But life is such a dishevelled production that it wasn't that way at all. We must have known each other five or six months at least before he ever gave me that suddenly attentive look—his blue eyes intent and also rather surprised—and asked me out to dinner. Understandable in the Protestant School Board, of course, if not at MGM. Lowly female teachers are rarely cosy with principals. Nothing, in fact, might ever have happened at all, if it hadn't been for a case of plagiarism in my class that I was too inexperienced to know how to handle. So I asked for an appointment with the principal. Miss Chew, his secretary, aged a hundred, gave me one with reluctance, and when Pat and I first were alone, it was over a Grade Ten copy of a *Reader's Digest* article on Mother Love. He was bored, by me and the article equally, preoccupied with a Board meeting due the next hour, and kept glancing at his watch.

But what an attractive creature I thought he was— Irish black hair and fair skin, heavy eyebrows meeting in a bar over very blue eyes; shoulders and chest heavy and legs short; a rather shy and tentative smile that showed crooked front teeth. The truth is, I thought him a very handsome man the first time somebody pointed him out on the platform at my first assembly. More truth is that I didn't need to see him at all about the *Digest* article—knew the Board policy on plagiarism quite well, and could have coped alone. Ah, well . . .

"Awfully sorry to be in such a rush, but this meeting . . . I'm sure if you give this boy a good stiff warning—first offender, after all; then of course if there's any trouble after that, send him straight to me."

Not named Eva for nothing, though. Got on a department committee; got elected junior staff representative on the Board; sat near him at meetings. Seconded one of his motions. That's romance in school-administration circles. Eventually he even asked me to lunch (in the cafeteria). Which I earned, believe me. Because he was president of the local branch, I endured cramps of boredom at meetings of the Humanities Society. Once I thanked the speaker for him. Don't ask me what I had in mind. At the time I was going out regularly with a plump, early-balding chap called Roger and even thinking vaguely I might marry him, because he had a lot of money. Everybody, including me, knew that Pat was married.

> *Old music-hall joke:*
> M.C.: "Miss 'Arriet 'Awkins will now sing Fythful and True."
> VOICE FROM THE GODS: " 'Arriet 'Awkins is a 'ore!"
> M.C.: "*Nevertheless,* Miss 'Arriet 'Awkins will sing Fythful and True."

So, nevertheless, when he asked me out to dinner at last (after a particularly long and stupefying Board meeting)—explaining in a rather nervous undertone that his wife was out of town—I accepted at once and scampered off to the Ladies', heart going pitty-pat, to make myself as magnetic as possible on such short notice. Not a bad-looking girl in those days, either—shingled, thick, goldy-brown hair cut in a straight bang, fresh skin, a good body with long, handsome legs, a tiny waist (oh me, that was long ago), and fashionably scanty breasts.

"Let's get as far as we can from the school," he said. "How about Chez Son Père?"

Fine with me. A zero evening, clear and blue as a plum, black downtown buildings cages of light, the air so cold it was still stinging when it got into our blood. Walked across the paved school courtyard to the parking lot with frost nipping our legs. Even inside his old Reo our breath came out white, and we laughed because our hands were too cold to hold a cigarette. That was when he first looked at me with that basic, direct, male look that says "I want you." As for me, I didn't know what I wanted, I only felt my blood singing.

Dinner, place very crowded and much Gallic din; hard to talk. Remember being secretly bored by a long discourse of his on boats—he kept a schooner-rigged sailboat for holidays. Loose thread on his stiff blue shirt-collar. Very beautiful hands with long fingers and oval nails, surprising with his rather stocky build.

Eventually our eyes met.

"Let's get out of here," he said abruptly.

Night very black and still, and burning with cold. He drove without a word up the mountain to the look-out, where all Montreal lovers still go, not to look at the view. Parked, lit cigarettes, pretended to study the opaque frost crystals on the car windows.

"My wife's left me, you know," he said suddenly. I looked at him. My heart had given a jerk of surprise.

"But probably you've heard. Everybody must know."

"I didn't. Nobody told me."

"She just—don't think this is self-pity, it's just that I'd like you to know. She went off to be with somebody else, that's all."

39

There was a lame pause. "I'm sorry."

"I'm sorry too. And that's the truth."

"How long were you—"

"Six years."

"Well, maybe she'll come back."

"I don't think so. She's in New York. He's a doctor there. She first went to him for warts on her feet." Suddenly he gave a loud snort of laughter. We'd had a bottle of wine with dinner, and two cognacs afterwards, and he was not perfectly sober. But I was. I smiled painfully as if I were the one hurting.

"No, she won't come back," he said.

He picked the cigarette out of my fingers and threw it away. Then he kissed me, his lips very tentative at first, almost shy, as if he were afraid I might rebuff him. The tip of his nose on my cheek was so cold I began to laugh, but he pulled my head back and kissed me again, confidently now, his tongue urging my mouth open. His adroit hand opened one or two buttons of my coat and he took my breast with a little groan of pleasure. Oddly enough, though all this was very pleasant, I felt no specific desire for him, only a glow of loving-kindness. Nor was he swept away himself. Soon he shifted away to sit behind the wheel again.

"And that, I guess, is enough of that," he said. "Where do you live?"

"Out in Montreal West."

"Alone?"

"No. With my parents."

He smiled and patted my cheek with one of those gestures of pure tenderness I would soon know too well. "I'll take you home now."

When we reached my street and the car was still, he hesitated an absent moment before opening the door, and in vague, reflected light from the dash, I saw his eyes guarded by their stiff, dark lashes, eyes dark and lonely, full of knowledge, compassion, and sorrow. It was like seeing the man's most private, inner self—and it woke up mine, mine that had been asleep for twenty-three years, to an astonished, apprehensive life.

"Pat—"

"Thank you for tonight."

A blank pause.

"Would you like to come in for coffee?"

"No thanks, my dear. It's late."

"Yes, I suppose it is."

"I'll see you to the door."

"Yes."

He kissed me briefly on the cheek and said good-night. I let myself in and crept upstairs. And lay awake a long time, tingling everywhere, in a whirl of confused, crazy hopes and other delusions. And that was, oh God, only the beginning.

Lying there in my basement bed, recalling all this, it occurred to me that a trip down memory lane had about as much romance in it as a monkey's quest for fleas—only once you begin to search you find too much to stop. I made a powerful effort to concentrate on anything else—The Suez Canal, for instance, or inflation. That didn't work, of course. Neither did counting the people I knew who had divorces or poodles or ulcers. No use at all.

More than three weeks went by before I saw Pat again. Every hour of it like a year. Time enough to live through all the degradations of love—the helpless expectation, the obsessive memories, the hungry waiting. And worst humiliation of all, the secret, motive-less joy. It was in that three-week gap I met Burt at somebody's engagement party. Very tall and thin, pale, narrow face topped with stiff, fair hair. I thought he looked like a man cut out of paper, but he was a surprisingly good dancer, and I annoyed Roger by fox-trotting with him a lot that evening.

Black March crawled away and wet April began. A farewell staff party for ancient Miss Chew, who had been handed on like an heirloom from principal to principal and was now, to everyone's relief, retiring at last. There she was in a stiff, new dress, grinning behind a huge corsage of yellow roses. The bristles on her chin were a bit tremulous, for this was in effect the end of her life, and even I was not too young and callous to recognize that. But for me the crowded hotel room, with its huge chandeliers, the noise, the rather bad cocktails, the speech presenting a gilt clock —all of it was only Pat in a grey suit with a red carnation in the buttonhole, giving La Chew a ceremonial kiss—no doubt her first, I muttered to May. He disappeared then in the crush, and before we could get away we found ourselves cornered by the staff bore— a fat man from the Maths Department with a strong Glasgow accent and a braying laugh. People melted away from his neighborhood as from the tinkle of a leper's bell, and for twenty minutes we were trapped.

Then, without warning, a hand took mine from behind and slipped up deliberately the full length of my bare arm. Pat's blue eyes looked at us all in austere official greeting. "Miss Daly, I'd like you to come over and meet a guest from the South Shore Board; maybe you could show him around the school tomorrow."

"Yes, of course," I said, and was at once extricated so swiftly and expertly I found myself out in the lobby before there was time to say another word.

"To hell with the South Shore Board," he said. "Feel like something to eat? Then get your coat and let's go."

Heart beating like a landed fish. Rain shimmering in the dark outside, long streamers of colour in the wet road. Through long arrows of rain we ducked into the car.

"Where would you like to go?"

"What about that little place Le Provençal?"

"No, we—I don't think much of it there."

"Oh." A barb of pain and anger deep in the flesh. For a minute I couldn't speak at all.

"Cheer up. The steak at Toby's is terrific." With lighthearted speed he threaded the Reo around a bumbling trolley car. "How have you been, anyway? Wasn't that a grim party? Poor old Chew, what a life she's given us; I had to sneak letters home to answer them my way. As for Dan Larsen before me, she gave him shingles and made him retire early, did you know that?"

No answer. I held back even the faintest twitch of a smile. He glanced sideways at me and dropped a little conciliatory pat on my hand. Suddenly truly angry, I said, "Where have you been all this time?"

At once his face darkened.

"Here and there. Spent a few days in Ottawa at a conference last week."

"Did you."

"Yes."

"Oh."

"What a damned silly question, darling. I've been in and out of hell, if you really want to know."

And looking at him, I saw he was telling the simple truth. Too sore yet to say a word, I laid my hand briefly on his knee for a message, and with relief saw his eyes begin to close in a smile.

"And we'll have a damned good bottle of burgundy with it," he said.

Afterwards all he said was, "A drink at my place?", and all I said was nothing. A new brick apartment block on a steep hill near the school. He glanced around swiftly for neighbours before we went in— and I swallowed that like medicine. It was the beginning of the end of being young; the sour fruit of the tree of knowledge.

Inside, books and a ukulele on the mantlepiece, and many crawling green vines and tree-like things in pottery tubs, all carefully tended, though the wife

43

had been gone several months now. He whisked away my coat, wound up a gramophone, and gave me a swift kiss on the neck to distract my gaze from this jungle. When I said, "What, no apples?" he didn't understand. Nor did he want to waste any time in idle chat. Before our drinks were half finished he was silently unhooking the black lace bodice of my dress and pushing up the short skirt to caress and admire my legs. "Oh, you are a pretty thing," he muttered. "A pretty, pretty thing."

I was so intact a virgin that it was a real surprise, even something of a shock, to find the position (on the sofa) so uncomfortable and undignified. The effort to conceal this seemed to leave no time to feel much pleasure at all. But it was lovely to lie naked with him; I fully intended to go through with it. Eyes closed (those damned plants), I laced my arms around his warm, square torso and waited.

"Pat, I love you with my whole heart," I said.

Well, it was that, or some technical difficulty he encountered at the same instant—I couldn't tell which; girls weren't at all well informed in those days—in any case, he stopped short.

"Oh, Jesus, darling—look, you've never done this before, have you?" He looked down into my face with troubled eyes.

"What difference does that make?"

"Quite a lot, really."

I didn't answer. Another minute and he had shifted himself away from me with a groan. "I don't know whether this makes me a heel or a hero," he said, and lay still. It was a full minute before I realized he was not going to complete the act.

"Try not to be sore at me, Eva. Or yourself either. It's just that I can't accept . . . it wouldn't be fair. I'm ten years older than you, and I know ten times as much about these things. One of them is that I have no business whatever messing up your life. You will marry someone as nice as yourself and have several babies and be happy. And right now I'm outside all that. Maybe I always will be."

He dried my eyes, carefully picked up the black wisp of my dress from the floor, and made me finish my drink. In a matter-of-fact way he climbed back into his own clothes and sat down across the room with a refilled glass for himself. For a while we said nothing more. Rain rattled the windows in gusts.

"Of course you find it hard to understand this," he said finally. "And it's damn hard to explain to a girl like you. But the truth is, if Lila came back tomorrow, I would be the happiest married man in creation. Does that make any sense? No questions I want to ask her. No complaints I want to make. None at all. I'm committed, you see, in the way that matters most. The only way that matters at all. Can you understand that?"

"Yes," I said hoarsely. "I know more about it than you think, because I've been honest with you too. Now I'm going home."

The dignity of this exit was slightly chipped by a long search for one of my shoes which had gotten inaccessibly kicked under the sofa; but eventually I was dressed and on the way home through sheets of pelting rain. We had nothing left to say to each other, and a grinding headache had begun behind my eyes. Furthermore, I had (did Isolde, I wonder, or Juliet ever?) a severe case of indigestion that racked me with hiccups. Dully I marvelled at Pat's serene expression; there was even a dry glint of humour in his eyes when he gave my shoulder a farewell squeeze.

"Good-night, dear. Take a teaspoonful of sugar for the hiccups, and go to sleep," he said.

It was the best possible advice, but of course I neither thanked him for it nor took it. The occasion seemed to me to call for long, silent hours of agonized weeping, and I duly spent them till day came. Then, with a head full of rocks and eyes swollen nearly shut, I got up and went to school to correct some exams that could perfectly well have waited. The truth was, I was afraid to stay in bed. It seemed to me I could easily lose the art of getting up altogether.

Vague sounds came down to me in my cave; a dim swaying like music under water. Pipes, furnace whirr, front-door bang. Voices. Wind. Taps running. Cats in the back lane yowling. No matter what the time or season, they carried out the raucous ritual of their sex lives. At least once, and generally oftener, every night, the dark was split by their shameless yells of lust and triumph. I'd learned to know one of them well from his favourite beat around the back-lane garbage tins; a randy old tom with one ear in rags, the other just a stump. Black coat battered and a raw sore on one flank; but he was lean, agile, indestructible. Something about him I rather liked. If that back door of mine hadn't been jammed, I might even have put out a few scraps, in spite of the way he broke up my sleep and intruded his vulgar voice into the memories of my great love. There was a certain male swagger hard to resist in those tattered whiskers. It was a sure thing he didn't feel apologetic or confused or analytical about the mounting of his many queens. Once he leapt onto my kitchen window-sill and stared in at me boldly, as at an equal. Wished he'd been around years earlier; I might have picked up a few useful tips and escaped a lot of misery.

The summer that followed certainly taught me plenty, though not nearly enough. I saw nothing whatever of Pat, and assured myself it was completely and finally over—whatever "it" might be—but I spent every second waiting. Just waiting, stubbornly and irrationally. In the centre, everything was concentrated on this, though the rest of me was very brisk and busy. I went to Europe for the first time, on a tour, with a lot of camera-carrying teachers. Wrote postcards in Paris, had dysentery in Athens—the standard tour. In London I met Roger, and in a hotel bedroom one night parted willingly enough with that long-preserved virginity, it being no longer a posession I prized at all. Afterwards I thought about the whole business with real indignation. "Is that all there is to it?" I thought incredulously. "Why, what a lot of liars people are—specially writers—to make anything so trivial seem the most earth-shaking experience possible. Why do none of them mention that ludicrous noise, or the man's comically vacant look of concentration? To think I've been brought up to believe a girl looked recognizably 'different' the next morning, and to accept my mother's phrase 'a good girl' as meaning a virgin!" All this rubbish made me feel extremely cross, and suspicious too, as if possibly a number of my other middle-class values might be just as unsound.

All the time, though, the waiting went on. Some kind of instinct told me to wait, and I did. Perhaps it was instinct, too, that taught me the meaner arts of strategy. At the first staff meeting of the new term, I chose a seat beside a notably handsome new teacher in Botany, introduced myself, and proceeded to dazzle him, all for Pat's benefit. I recognized *him* only after a while and with a distant nod. Grimly gratified when he came up after the meeting, looked at me irritably from the blue eyes, and said, "Can I offer you a lift home?"

"Oh!—yes, thanks."

In the car he gripped the wheel before starting and stared at me.

"Have a good summer?" he asked.

"Yes, very nice. I went on that Association tour. What about you?"

"I was out on the west coast mostly—my two brothers live out there."

"I see."

"Who was that clown with you at the meeting? New, isn't he?"

"Oh, that's Tom West, in Botany. Good-looking, isn't he? And very bright."

"No doubt. I suppose you wouldn't consider—you wouldn't come and have a drink with me somewhere?"

"No, thanks, Pat, I wouldn't."

"All right." He turned the ignition on and began to back out of the parking lot, his face quite expressionless.

"How's your new secretary working out?"

"Oh, fine. English girl. Very capable." He gave me a sidelong wink. "Quite good-looking, too. And very bright."

"Good luck," I said viciously.

He stiffened, but his voice was controlled. "Don't be like that. It doesn't suit you, Eva."

Ashamed, I twisted my hand into his and muttered "Sorry. Really, Pat. I'm sorry, and I'd love a drink."

It was nearly an hour, though, sitting side by side on barstools at Mother Martin's, before the wary look in his eyes faded. But I saw to it that our knees touched and our hands, and the martinis were a considerable help. Eventually, looking at my breasts, he said, "Would you like some dinner?"

"Oh, I would, but—well . . . "

"Why not? Good seafood place just across the road."

Lowered eyes. Fingers toying with toothpick. "No, I don't think I'd better . . . thanks, but I think I'd better get on home."

"Why?"

Looked him squarely in the eyes. "Afraid not to, Pat. I can't get mixed up with you again—just can't afford it. It hurts too much. I care too much. That's why. Now let's go."

He drove me home looking thoughtful. Outside the house, oblivious to passers-by, he took my mouth in a long and potent kiss. Then he let me go. "You beautiful bitch," he muttered. "Go home then." And I had

48

the grace to feel corrupt and ashamed in my triumph afterwards. Because the truth was, it was the first day of my period, and that was really why I wouldn't spend the evening with him. The rest was strategy. And successful, even if he did partly see through it.

Less than two weeks later, at a conference in Ste. Agathe of the Humanities Society—most of it there for the same purpose (ah, humanity)—Pat and I became lovers. As the saying goes. And it doesn't go far. Like so many long-anticipated things, bed for us was something of a disappointment. But that didn't matter. The one important thing was that, rattling home in the train afterwards, I could think, "He's mine now." There was deep satisfaction in that.

A week or more went by before I saw him again. Rather glad of that. Time to forget some of the less attractive details and remember the rest . . . things like lying propped up naked on pillows later, drinking brandy in the dark. I felt serene, happy, and smug. But not for long.

He came up to my classroom early, before the first bell of the day. The sight of him at the door was a surprise, and the look of him a shock. He had dark pouches under his eyes, blotches showed on his cheeks, his heavy shoulders sagged.

"What's the matter?" I asked, frightened.

"Are you by yourself?" He closed the door behind him carefully. "I had to tell you this right away. Lila's come back. She was in the apartment when I got home last night."

No comment at all occurred to me.

"Well, I had to tell you. Because, my dear, what I told you about Lila still goes. I'm truly sorry . . . I didn't know anybody could feel like such a louse, if that's any help. But there it is."

"Yes. I see."

"No hard feelings, I hope, Eva, dear. Because you've been very sweet to me, and I'm grateful."

"Yes . . . no . . ."

Soon, to my profound relief, he went away. After that, I seemed to stare for days and days on end down into a fathomless pit, and long for it to swallow me. As far as I could tell, the world had ended. But women, by their inner chemistry, are resilient creatures: with men around, they develop this talent out of grim necessity. The time for my period approached and passed, and though we had taken several different kinds of anxious precautions, I began to count days and speculate, and the numb misery began to lift a little. What if—what if . . .

I couldn't shut out all sorts of fantasies, vague but vivid, more real than reality. A child of Pat's . . . God, my poor parents . . . what would he do? Where would I go? Could the two of us . . . ? Even at the worst, if he persisted in loyalty to his wandering Lila, I would have his child—perhaps a son, his son—and that would be mine. All mine, no matter what.

But I had to talk to someone; so May and I had lunch, in the cafeteria, because her job in the school library provided only a meagre hour and there was no time to go anywhere else for privacy.

"I have this damn meeting tonight and I can't talk to you on the phone with Mum and Dad there. . . ."

"Don't talk so fast," advised May, "and grab that corner table."

"You know Pat Devlin's wife, don't you?"

"Oh. Well, yes. Used to. Lila and I went to school together. Why?"

"What's she like?"

"Odd. But you must know that."

"She's come back to him—did you hear?"

"Oh, yes, I heard." She was careful not to look at me. May was the best possible friend, perceptive but always careful of privacy. Now all she said was, "I wonder how he feels about that?"

"He's delighted."

"The poor bastard."

"But is she clever or gorgeous or what? I've never met her, you know. She must be pretty magnetic."

"Well, not to me she wasn't. Just odd. With whiskers she'd look exactly like a cat. At school she was all over the place—brilliant at some things and a moron at the rest. She'd try anything. Smoked a cigar, stole a watch from Birks . . . terribly easily bored, restless, quite neurotic. Her parents were rich Americans, divorced and all that. She ran away to marry Pat—somebody told me she chose some place in the South in case they ever wanted a quickie divorce."

"Practical girl," I said grimly.

"People either couldn't stand Lila or they adored her, no middle of the road. I couldn't stand her."

"Neither can I."

Five days later my fantasies ended abruptly, and I had no more questions to ask anybody.

But there had been enough comfort in May's conversation to last through that whole winter. A dogged, stubborn hopefulness kept me going from one white week to the next, a grim willingness to wait. If she left him once, she might again. She just might. Unstable as mercury from the sound of her. He might, even yet . . . if I could just hang on and wait. . . .

Burt settled down to a plodding, determined courtship that winter, and though I knew him no better on closer acquaintance, I hadn't the energy to shake him off. Every Saturday night he took me to a movie, and we had a late dinner afterward, always at the same restaurant. He was like that. When it was time to say good-night, he always kissed and fondled me for the same brief time and then always stopped decisively, with obvious and painful difficulty. But he was the sort of man who would despise himself for "going the whole way" (his wonderful phrase) with a girl he intended to marry. He made it clear he wanted to marry within a year and live in a bungalow on the suburban edge of the city, and then have five children, three of them boys. My parents admired Burt greatly. I did too, in a way; he appeared to me the most predictable and simplified human being in the world. The only surprising and inexplicable detail was that for some reason I found him sexually exciting, in spite of the fact that, if anything, I rather disliked his cold, blond leanness and his pale eyes. Many other things about him failed to charm, too. He was studying at night to become a chartered accountant; he was a Baptist and a teetotaller, and he liked football and knew every one of its rules. Incredible, but with all this he could make my blood pound with a touch.

And then—at last—the reward of patience. March. A tremor of rain.

Staff room gossip. "She's left him *again*, can you believe it? Someone told me that her lawyer wrote and . . . they say he . . . "

I walked all the way home, breathing the tender green haze on the old city trees, the blue air, the puff of warmth and moisture from wet earth in gardens. Next morning one of the secretaries appeared at the office door, collecting.

"It's Mr. Devlin. He's in hospital, poor man. We thought a big basket of spring flowers—"

"What's wrong with him?"

"Well, nobody seems to know exactly. Some say he has a bad back, it needs an operation. But it sounds like a nervous breakdown or something like that to me. I think Katy Watson, that stuck-up secretary, knows, but of course she won't say. Poor soul, he's sure had enough problems at home. His wife up and left him *again*, did you know? She must be out of her head, he's so cute with those blue eyes. Anyhow, we thought it would cheer him up, a few flowers—"

"Maybe it would, but—actually I'm stony broke today, Doris. Sorry, but you'd better count me out."

No, it wouldn't do to have my name on that get-well card, even if all he had was a slipped disc. So the time for strategy had come round again, and I kept on waiting, alert and stupid as a dog at a vacant rat-hole. Sent him, finally, a carefully casual little note, which he didn't answer. At intervals during that summer I asked casually of this one and that how he was getting on. Told Burt I was sorry, but . . . Offended (after all those movies—a long investment, after all), he disappeared. Relief. Began the new school year with zest. Pat came back to work looking strained and white. He never called me or sought me out at the school. Weeks and weeks went by like that. A bad sort of fatigue began to draw at me, as I began slowly to understand. The worst moments of all were those rare ones when he paused in the hall or on the stairs for a friendly word or two, and then hurried on about his business with a cheerful smile.

For a long time before I could afford to admit it, I knew the truth. There was no real surprise in the final sentence—Katy Watson in the staff lounge, showing her engagement ring, a pretty garnet in a circle of little diamonds, and chatting in her high, English voice about taking Pat home in August to meet her parents.

And so, when Burt asked abruptly, after calling in to see Dad one Sunday after his first heart attack, "When are you going to marry me?" I said, "In August, if you like."

He turned so white I thought he might fall down.

"Do you mean it?"

"Yes. Do you?"

He looked at me hard out of his rather prominent pale-blue eyes, but asked no further questions, then or later. Burt was not totally without imagination.

"Well," I thought, "at least I'll have this." It seemed to me extremely important not to be left with nothing. A husband, five children, and a bungalow in Pointe Claire were all good things and worth having. So at the altar I listened with approval to all the exhortations about having and holding, and answered "I will" with a clear voice. My mother cried like a fountain; so did May. But I never shed a tear.

And on my wedding night I had cause to regard Baptists, teetotallers, and chartered accountants with a certain new respect. That too was worth having. Or so I thought, at the time.

Funny, after living all those years with Burt's clocks, not to know when I woke up what the time was, or even the day. But I felt a lot better. A spot of research into the past seemed to have helped somehow. Now that was over, I felt weak and tottery, but very hungry. All that was left in the old woman's cupboard was a heel of bread and a bit of tea; I had those and then slowly got dressed. I had shrunk considerably, which was not a bad thing. A twinkle of cold sun at the window like a wink said, Come out, so, padded in sweaters and moving ponderously as a diver, I crept out into the bright day. The first icy mouthful of air was a shock and then a pleasure, like a gulp of gin. I had eighty-nine cents and big plans to buy a gourmet lunch of frozen chicken pie.

Conservative progress and occasional pauses brought me to the corner Chinese grocery. Another little rest by the door and my eye caught the crossed metal snap of a little change purse half-hidden under dead leaves and rubbish at an angle of the step. Retrieved it with a grunt, and fumbled it open. Seven dollars in bills inside, a stamp, two bus tickets, and a scrap of old paper in a separate compartment. What a bit of luck. Couldn't stop smiling as I bought a piece of steak, several tins of things, fresh bread, and a packet of candy. There was even enough to buy sherry, though that would have to wait—I was too tired to walk that far yet.

Home again joggety-jog, with only one or two stops to breathe on the way. Fellow in the long overcoat I've seen around even paused to ask in broken English if he could help me. Afterwards realized he was the old boy who lived somewhere in the house. Wished he hadn't stopped; it's depressing to look as needy as all that. However. Made it home all right without help, and sat down awhile, bag and all, to wheeze and rest the feet and other friends. Shoe predicament insoluble, it would seem: old ones a scandal, new ones a torment.

Inspected the purse again, at leisure, to gloat. Two bus rides, a nice little present. Opened the bit of folded paper. It was a note that read "Dear J., bless you for everything." I didn't throw it away. The money was one thing, but a message is a message and has value.

The next day I shuffled out cheerfully to buy the sherry. A newspaper on top of a trash-bin startled me by pointing out it was half-past November. My conscience twinged so sharply then that I stopped in a phone booth on the way home and called Neil.

"Do you realize it's been nearly two *weeks*?" he said in the high voice of outrage. "Mother, you just don't seem to realize—"

"Well, I've been down with something. Call it flu. Couldn't ring you till now. Anyhow, you'll have to get over worrying about me, dear. I'm fine now and I don't need a thing—that's all I called to say. How's Kim?"

"Oh, all right, but she's gone all moody and difficult lately. She's upset about you, for one thing. Look, Mum, I want to see you. Meet me somewhere. We simply can't leave things like this."

"Of course we can, Neil. There's nothing to argue about as far as I'm concerned. Has your father agreed to let me have a little money every month, or not?"

"Well, no—he—"

"All right. I didn't really expect it."

"Mum, he's in a bad way. Terrible pain. The doctor's put him on some sort of injections, cortisone, I think, and a V.O.N. comes in every day, but—"

"Well, I'm sorry. But it doesn't change anything. He's been on cortisone before and it relieves him. He'll be all right. If he's not willing to help me, that's fair enough, I suppose. I'm not willing to help him either."

A silence. Then he said heavily, "I honestly can't understand this. After all this time . . . and you don't seem to care at all. About any of us. Mum, I think you need expert help. Don't you see, it isn't normal, any of this. You're not yourself. Even your voice sounds different—sort of far away and neutral."

"Does it?"

"Dear, you've had some kind of breakdown, you must realize that. We all want to take care of you. A psychiatrist—"

"Nice of you, Neil, but no. Does it occur to you it may be a good thing to be broken down? You're right, I feel different. Neutral, if you like. But I honestly don't need anybody or anything. That may not seem normal to you, but it seems like the beginning of wisdom to me. Or something. Sorry if it sounds bad . . . or sick. But do try not to bother yourself about it. Give Kim and the boys my love, and be sure to tell her I'm fine, won't you? Call you again one of these days."

And in some haste I rang off. Struggled out of the phone booth with my parcel and hurried away as if his solicitude and anxiety were threats that might catch me and pull me back. As they might well do.

Hurrying reminded my legs they still got tired quickly, so I soon had to slow down, and even then I felt so fagged that I took a short-cut through the lanes to get back to the MacNab house quicker. Off the streets, in cement-paved alleys where nobody but a stray kid and dog or two loitered, I felt better. It cheered me to remember that my pension cheque had arrived that morning at the new address, so I could pay the rent and still feel agreeably rich for a day or two. Clutched the sherry in its paper bag with care: lots of loose stones and rubbish in these lanes. Would have a shot when I got home, to celebrate. What?—breakdown or build-up? Well, what I'd wanted to say to Neil was that maybe they amount to the same thing.

Near MacNab's brick rear, I navigated carefully around the crowd of garbage tins. Near one of them lay a small plant in a smashed clay pot. It couldn't have been there long, because it clung still to its clod of earth, and the leaves had just begun to wilt. Rather nice, glossy leaves, elegantly narrow. Finding that purse the day before had sharpened my eye, or I might never have noticed it. Nice to find things. Specially things nobody else seemed to want.

With a quick glance round to make sure no psychiatrists were looking, I scooped up the plant and its earth, a messy handful, and bundled myself inside with it. Anybody watching would have thought me guilty—or crazy. But it was a good plant, too good to throw away. Put it into a jar or tin and give it a drink (then have one myself), and it would do well in the sun over the kitchen sink. Maybe one of these days I might find a whole pot for it. Surprising what you could find if you looked. People threw away the oddest things. Imagine throwing away a plant, when you think of all the dead things carefully kept, like photo albums and hats and furs. . . .

No, from now on I would keep a sharp eye out for things to find. A hobby. Therapy, Neil.

No doubt there was something wrong—even sick— in a woman who could discard such items as a husband's pain and a son's worry, and adopt instead a mute green creature with roots for brains. I didn't even know the thing's name. But that was why the life of it was so satisfactory. It was anonymous and impersonal, both great things.

I poured out some sherry and looked into its golden

57

eye. Good-bye, Burt. Good-bye, Neil. Bless you for everything, and good-bye.

The plant looked in good heart, packed into an old soup tin and well watered. My wine glowed all the way down. I looked around and felt grand and snug, wonderfully alone.

A few days later the sky opened and snow began to cataract down on the city. As dusk came on, a raging wind drove the soft fall into blind, stinging clouds. My little radio reported paralysing traffic tie-ups, hundreds of commuters stranded, cars abandoned all along Sherbrooke Street. Even down in my cave, I huddled into several sweaters; the wind hissed and banged against the windows and a little drift of dry snow even managed to invade the bathroom sill.

I was glad I'd done my bit of shopping earlier and had enough in the house to eat for awhile, because without my winter boots I might have to stay inside for days. However, this didn't bother me much. Had recently used my two bus tickets to visit the public library at Atwater and brought home a nice armful of books—things I'd wanted to read for years, or re-read, and somehow never got round to. *War and Peace*, for instance, and *Middlemarch*, Thurber's *Is Sex Necessary?*, Chaucer and *King Lear* and *Madame Bovary*. Felt like a millionaire with these chaps in a row by my bed. Not that it turned out to be escape literature, though. A nice cosy read may have been what I had in mind, but it's not what I got. A third eye seemed to have opened somewhere in my head, in fact, and I saw things in these books I'd never perceived before—things that were far from soothing. I guess Auden was right when he said a real book reads us. I'd read *Lear* before, for instance, and never found anything there except an irritating old bugger who caused a lot of trouble. But now I saw that what most writers appear to brood on most is the knotted-together web of responsibility and concern that holds people together in society. All my books seemed to be about what private people do to public things like duty and responsibility. Made me feel literature uncomfortably close to life, for the first time. The last thing I wanted was to know that Emma was me; and this was a hell of a night to be reading about Lear naked in the storm. Poor crazy old thing, throwing away everything he had; the whole universe punished him to death for that. I suppose he became human along the way, but was it worth it? And what if, like me, he'd become detached and neutral—not more human but less? Would that make his story a comedy instead of a tragedy?

Around eleven o'clock the wind seemed worse than ever, and I padded out to the kitchen to see whether snow was getting in at the window there. Not much was, but it was so cold even the bugs had retired. Peering out between my hands to inspect the storm, I made out a rounded shape pressed to the glass outside, and when the current gust subsided, recognized the black tom of the lane crouching there, not engaged tonight in *amour*, only trying with some difficulty to survive. I forgot Lear thankfully and squinted out again, wondering why the stupid cat chose this exposed place to huddle in, when he might have found a cranny out of the wind. Thought cats were so shrewd. But maybe too much fornication had dulled his wits. Or weakened his legs. I tapped the glass sharply.

"Go round the other side of the house, you sex maniac," I told him. The tapping roused him; he half stood up, and then I saw why he was in no mood to travel; one of his front paws was a shapeless mass—crushed by a car, perhaps. Poor old tom. He'd never make it through the night, and he seemed to know it. He looked in at me, straight in the eyes—a realist's hard look that asked for nothing and promised nothing, only said, "I have no hope."

I went and got my coat. Not a cat-lover by any means, but I'd never be able to sleep with that poor wretch dying right at my elbow. The cellar door giving onto the lane outside was jammed, so after a short grapple with it that failed, I went upstairs, let myself out into the maelstrom, and with difficulty began to flounder through the drifts of snow at the side of the house. It was incredibly cold. The wind sucked away my breath maliciously and tore at my hair. The deep snow gulped my legs to the knee. On a patch of exposed ground freakishly left bare, a slick of ice brought me down with a loud, low-comedy thump. So winded I couldn't get up for a minute, and what's more, in the shock I'd wet my pants. Even Lear didn't lose that much dignity. "Go on back in, you lunatic," I told myself angrily.

But having made it this far, I thought I might as well go on. A few more yards and through the whirlwind I could see the tom huddled against the window. When I managed to get hold of him in half-frozen hands, he snarled and hissed, the ungrateful bastard, and tore the front of my coat besides, with the claws he could still use. By the time I'd struggled back into the house and got him downstairs, we hated each other as if we'd been acquainted for years.

I dumped him in the kitchen while I got into some dry pants and stockings, and when I went back, he snarled from the remotest corner he could find. Offered him a bowl of warm milk, but he wouldn't touch it. His coat was staring, the smashed paw bled oozily onto the linoleum. When I got my thickest towel and dried him a bit, he snarled again, but common sense or exhaustion made him accept the favour. Now I looked at him more closely, it seemed improbable that he'd survive the night after all; he crouched there on the floor, eyes half closed, with a look of defeat.

"Well, it's up to you now," I told him. "Cheer up, old Romeo. Never say die." To that end I made him up a bed with a couple of towels on my new extravagance—a cut-rate drugstore hot-water bottle, which I'd planned to use myself that night to defy the foul fiend.

He crept up and crouched on this eventually, with only a perfunctory snarl or two, and seemed to doze. After an interval (when I was safely out of the room) he even lapped a bit of the milk. But his breathing was wheezy. Pneumonia would probably get him, even if nothing else did. And me too, in all likelihood, I thought with a shiver. Nothing more could be done for old tom, so I crept into bed. Dozed off soon. Storm still yelling and banging around in a tantrum out there. Toward daybreak I woke suddenly to wonder where it had all gone. The wind had died at last, and there wasn't a murmur in the whole paralyzed, shrouded city. Only from the kitchen came a fitful, hoarse, rasping purr.

When you're snowbound and have a stamp, it begins to seem necessary to write a letter. For a while, though, I couldn't decide to whom. It would have been nice to write to Kim; always easy to be close and frank and natural with her, in spite of our relationship and the half-century gap in our ages. We'd never tried to force each other into roles; it was always possible to talk or be as companionable in silence, and we never trespassed on each other's sensitive areas, because we had the same ones. But a letter was different; language on paper becomes so formalized and self-conscious; so public, somehow. Kim might even feel she ought to show it to her parents. Certainly they would consider it addressed more to them than to her. So not Kim. As for Burt, what could I possibly send him but silence? And Pat? What a weird notion. He would have forgotten my very name years and years ago. And all I could say to him, anyway, was the sort of thing never said in letters: "It was only vanity. Also, of course, vexation of spirit.

But never love." Never, though it took me forty years to realize that. And I was less prepared now than I ever was before to say what love is, so there wasn't much point in writing him at all.

"Sincerely not yours: Eva."

No; there was only one person I could perhaps say something to in a letter.

Dear May,

I have gone underground. Perhaps it wouldn't occur to them, they are both so literal, but just possibly Neil or Burt has been in touch with you, full of indignation and righteous wrath. Because I ran away and am hiding. Are you shocked? No, you always had too much sense of humour to be shocked at anything. Which is the chief reason I always liked you so much. Of course, to be fair, they can't afford to see anything funny in their mother and wife behaving in this crazy, stubborn way. But though you and I were so close, we could always laugh at each other; there was always enough detachment for that. Will you ever forget how we met at the school dance, the one when that Chemistry man was your date, and he'd given you the most enormous corsage of blue, red, and yellow flowers all wound up in broad pink ribbon. It was so superbly hideous that the minute our eyes met we both became victims of suppressed hysterics and had to retire to the Ladies' for half an hour.

But it always was the thing I admired most about you—the detachment that made life a joke to you so much of the time. It kept you safe and made you happy walking in your chosen, narrow way. I used to think, rather enviously, it was not being married that made it possible for you to be so serene. My life with Burt seemed so chaotic, painful, and raw by comparison, and I lost the art of laughing very soon. That's why, you see, this underground place of mine that I've found seems like such an Eden: is it possible that being turned out of paradise is heaven?

It's the first privacy, really, for me, ever. A grown-up daughter still living at home with her parents has no real privacy. There wasn't much, either, in the competitive mill of teaching, and less in the race of sex—no time in all that for any real aloneness or detachment, God knows.

As for marriage, what can one say too devastating about its awful proximities and involvements? (And rewards, of course.) Or motherhood with its boring, exhausting servitude? (And even better rewards?) The whole thing is just servitude to some enormous machine. And now I'm free. Alone. Hidden down here. Marvellous.

Remember that awful girl with spots at high school—Blossom?—and how we had fits after she told us that music was the true meaning of life, and then we found out all she could play was a tune called "Whispering Hope" on the G string of her violin? Well, I have a fellow-feeling these days with old Bloss. Almost as pretentious with all my words, and every bit as ridiculous. A beginner at seventy, an amateur of the rawest sort.

But it's rejecting so much I once valued that I think is so important. And for that you have to be alone. Make yourself alone, that is. Leave all you have and go underground. Of course it's squalid here. Ugly, uncomfortable. Not respectable. Or moral. Or "Normal". It's a totally selfish state of being, negative, even destructive. Don't ask me what can come of it. "Come, Sweet Death" was Blossom's second tune, remember. But I'm living.

Or am I in the grip of some kind of aberration? If it is, you'll understand it. How I'd like to talk to you, one of our long matters I used to enjoy so much. Your talent was for marginal comment on solemn subjects like Art or Moral Re-Armament which took place without words. You could turn the bath taps on with your toes, and play "La Ci Darem la Mano" by blowing into empty bottles, and knacks like these make me feel you would have the right perspective on my little adventure.

I won't see you again, my dear, but here is this letter with love.

Folded the page up carefully. And then, for some reason, put my head down and bawled, hard, for the first time since all this began.

It was days before the city dug out from the great drifts glittering like salt in an arctic sun. Meanwhile there was frozen silence and stillness everywhere. My place was more subterranean than ever with every window cataracted; I had to keep lights on all day, and it got hard to remember when night stopped and day began.

The old tom was glad enough in this interval to doze and recuperate. For diversion he licked the healing paw and hissed at me if I trespassed too near. When he could limp efficiently, he used a bit of plant earth I put out for him on newspaper, but he did this with an air of condescension, and ate what I provided only when I was out of the room, in case I should think him sentimental. But we were cooped up there together so long, I was glad of even his dour company. Quite normal people, after all, talk to cats where they wouldn't have a word to say to a bit of ivy in a pot.

Food supplies ran very low. No milk for tom eventually. Then, at last, Findlay's shovel flashed, a feeble, valiant banner in the pale sunshine, and a hole appeared in the white mask at the bathroom window.

Tom yelled at me imperiously, and I managed, by standing in the tub and whacking the window-frame, to open a space wide enough to let him wriggle out. Off he hopped into the snowy day with a jaunty switch of the tail, and never said good-bye. Sensible creatures, cats. No point, really, in gratitude.

He left me with a bit of wanderlust myself, so I bundled up well and ventured an excursion to buy food. Outside, the light was one great dazzle and with the zero wind it all but blinded me. Felt disturbingly insecure because of this and other problems—no sand had yet been laid on the side streets and it was murderously slippery underfoot, specially for a fat old woman without any snowboots. Twice I fell, not lightly, and tore down the hem of my coat; the second time my bag of groceries fell too, and tins rolled off briskly in various directions, to the loud delight of some teen-aged louts on the corner. By the time I got home, a very unpleasant fit of the trembles was on me, and it took quite a while to wear off. The fact was, for the first time I was afraid. In Montreal, winter is the only season. The streets might well stay like this till the end of March. If I couldn't get out to shop and so on, then I couldn't stay independent, and would have to admit defeat. Accept the end of it all. And all because I had no goddam boots!

The problem nagged and nagged me. I slept badly. Appetite disappeared. The row of books looked at me primly in their neat, unanimous row. "Well," they said, "How about it? *Is* no man an island? Is freedom bootless?" I thought and thought till my ears ached, but there just wasn't any solution. I had not quite four dollars to spare for essential food till my next cheque, and that would not begin to buy boots. Getting to the Salvation Army second-hand place (even if I knew where it was) would cost bus fare—sixty cents more. A bargain basement would have cheap rubbers or those plastic things to pull over shoes, but there was no warmth in them, and they were slippery too; no use at all. If only Burt had been the kind of easygoing husband with charge accounts here and there, I could have used one, but he'd always refused to have any at all; said they encouraged impulse-buying. Good old Burt, always so right.

No, there just wasn't any answer I could see. Morale sank to zero. I listened to a lot of FM music, but no inspiration, practical or otherwise, came of it. For the first time this total isolation of mine seemed rather silly: if there'd been anyone to talk to, perhaps an idea might have occurred; naturally the vine and the cockroaches had nothing useful to suggest. Brooded in great gloom till groceries got very low again—so low it was apparent I'd soon have to surrender. Of course, I could have gone home and *taken* my boots—but there was no use kidding myself I'd ever be able to get away again, not with Burt there filling the place up with suffering and reproaches. Those clocks with prim hands over their eyes would reclaim me, the spinet desk would need polishing, there would be letters for me and my best red wool back from the cleaner's . . . the world can't end twice.

The only practical alternative was a call to Neil— an appeal for help. He'd never refuse a few dollars— no need to agitate him by explaining what for. That would mean seeing him, though. And that was as bad, somehow, as the thought of going back to N.D.G. I'd mended the ripped-down hem of my coat, but tom's damage to the front was incurable, and flung-up slush from a car one mild day had stained part of the skirt with salt so badly that sponging wouldn't move it. And even if I could afford it, how could the thing go to the cleaners unless I slept there? I just couldn't let Neil see me looking like this. It was different before, deterioration hadn't really set in then, and I had more confidence, too. My old skin still fitted, somehow. But it made me writhe to think he would feel sorry for me; also that he'd have that satisfaction people get when they pity those who deserve their problems. I felt as if I'd pay any price but that.

Eventually, one bright morning, I heard a light rapping noise that brought me in a hurry to the kitchen window in my nightgown. It was water dropping from above in long silver flashes: the sun was melting the fur ledge of snow on window-sills overhead. My heart gave a jump. If it were that mild, I could go out. Even with my talent, it would be hard to fall down in slush. Waited impatiently till noon. Excited, got dressed and stepped out, breathing in the wet, fresh air with greed. The streets were now a mush of sand, salt, and melting snow; walking was quite easy, though of course it completed the murder of the poor old shoes.

Bought as big a bag of provender as I could carry, and then decided to go home the long way, past the shops on Lagauchetière, because the main streets were almost bare and by now my feet were aching wet. It was there I passed a shop full of boys' sweaters and socks and shoes—and pulled up short. The shoes were the canvas kind with thick, ribbed rubber soles. If only—of course it was ridiculous. You couldn't wear shoes like that, boys' white running-boots—they'd look absurd. But if that didn't matter, why couldn't you? Lace 'em up tight to fit, put a pair of thick socks inside for warmth. I still had my four dollars. The ticket said "Aubaine: $3.49." I went in. Pretended to look at sweaters, then asked carelessly about the shoes. Yes, they had the right size. For my grandson, I said, and fumbled out the money hastily, as if I were doing something illegal or immoral.

Well, even if I never wear them, I argued, they'll be there, insurance against being trapped indoors by weather. It ate me, though, all those artful dodges in the shops, playing games with my own pride, like a fool . . . and it was impossible actually to picture myself wearing such things. From a shabby but forgettable figure, I would graduate to a freak overnight

67

in those shoes. Surely I could never do that. But I hung onto the box as I passed a trash basket that seemed to want it, and once home, I hid the shoes at the back of a cupboard and tried to forget them.

I would just pray for a mild minter, that's all. There was something almost obscene in the thought of my narrow, elegant feet walking the streets in a kid's white sneakers. No, I couldn't do that, no matter what.

Funny, but those shoes reminded me, for some reason, of my cousin Midge's white graduation dress, which I also wouldn't wear. But I had a stronger character at seventeen, and didn't.

"Mother, I'm not going to the graduation."

She looked at me in astonishment. "Not going! But everyone will be there!" For my mother, I thought irritably, the one safe rule amid life's bewilderments was to do what everybody else did. She was an intensely practical woman, for whom appearance and reality were the same thing. Her answer to everything was Conform. Accept. Join. Merge with the crowd. And so my brother and I wore Red River outfits in winter and Scout and Guide and school uniforms, and were indistinguishable from anybody else—a triumph of patient management on her part, because we were both stubborn resisters, and such disguises cost a lot—too much on my father's almost tragically small salary. She spent most of her time, as a result, mending and making over clothes for us that had belonged to our older cousins. Perhaps that was why so many of her metaphors had to do with clothing. "He's not cut out for it," she'd say, or "That won't wash." It didn't occur to me for years afterwards, of course, that she knew perfectly well clothing itself was a metaphor. Now she sat frowning over tucks in Midge's frilly white dress for me to wear at the graduation ceremony.

"No, I'm not going."

"But why ever not, Eva?"

"The whole thing is silly. Just a lot of dull speeches." Wisely, Mother made no attempt to dispute the truth of this. She simply tightened her mouth and repeated, "Everybody will be there."

"But I won't."

She took a few stitches in silence.

"It's not as if you had nothing suitable to wear. This dress is real *peau de soie;* you'll look lovely in it."

"No, I won't. You know Midge's things look awful on me."

"Nonsense," Mother said comfortably. She thought she understood now. Nature had played a nasty prank on Midge at puberty, turning a dainty little girl into a lowering, cubic adolescent. And, as both of us knew, Mother was not expert enough to take in those broad dresses of hers so they ever really looked well on me. However, they looked well enough at a glance, and in Mother's view, nothing more was necessary. White silk and frills were what innocent young girls wore to graduate in. Here they were for me. Why was I being so unreasonable?

"I'm not going," I repeated.

"I will speak to your father, then."

This meant handing me over to arguments from the opposite viewpoint—a technique that had never failed up to now. For my father was a mild, scholarly man, his mind always absorbed in the abstract. Appearance and reality had little or no connection for him. Yet he and Mother agreed perfectly on all major aspects of bringing up their children, even though each reached his conclusions by different reasoning. He looked at me now through his reading spectacles, which enlarged his eyes so that they were like two vague fish nosing the glass.

"What's all this about the graduation?"

"I'm not going, Daddy. It's a bore and pointless. I'm

going on to teachers' training; it's not as if this were the end of my education."

"No," he agreed.

"Well, then. Tell Mother to stop nagging me."

"But it is a ceremony, Eva. Ceremonies always have meaning."

"Not this one."

Once more the twin fish rose to the surface in mild query. "Mm. Speeches and things; I see what you mean. But there's a dance afterwards, isn't there?"

And so Father also thought he understood. Of course, no boy had asked me to the dance, because I had spent the last two years in a state of scornful academic supremacy, despising boys, writing plays in secret, and making arrangements to be a genius. Very naturally, the few boys I knew shunned me like a cobra.

"I'm not going to the dance, Dad. Silly waste of time. And that's final; just please tell Mother to leave me alone, will you? I am *not* going."

He was a kind man and let the subject drop. I loved my father deeply and often hurt him with my unkindness. Now he'd come a lot closer than Mother had to guessing my real reason, and so I had to punish him with bad temper and stubbornness. But on graduation night, Midge's white frills hung in the cupboard and I went to bed early with a volume of Pirandello, and tasted triumph. I had won a not-insignificant victory— my first over the world, the flesh, and my parents. What a pity such victories are so inconclusive. Here I was now, for instance, with these damn boys' sneakers, fighting on the other side, for I wore them of course, just days later.

What an almighty shock! I really thought I'd have a heart attack. The noise alone—like an avalanche. And how did I ever in the world come to leave that door at the top of the stairs unlocked? Always so important and satisfactory to lock that door and have my underground apartment completely to myself. I could not possibly have forgotten to lock it; yet, somehow or other, I must have. They say there are no accidents; sneaky old subconscious always up to its tricks—but mine would never do a stupid thing like that. I came in, after a little shopping trip, at dusk, unlocked my door behind the stairs, stepped down and locked it again after me, just as I always do. Surely? No one else had a key except the MacNabs to let in the meter men, and they never forgot anything, always scrupulously locked up everything after themselves . . . but I couldn't have forgotten. Not possibly.

Well, lately, let's face it, I have been just a bit woolly-minded—left my parcel on the grocery counter a few days ago, and had to go back for it; another day, put my change into a coat pocket and thought I'd lost it. Getting ancient and vague. Forgot because I'm so busy remembering these days—things and people now vanished like shadows on water, but still dimensional, moving around in the cinerama of memory. My father, for instance. He's been buried for thirty years now, but I was sure I saw him on the street the other day in his white scarf and long dark winter overcoat. That's because he's been on my mind so much lately—can't think why—even in dreams he keeps on turning up, always in that long last illness, frail and helpless and pitiful. Was thinking of him when I came home from shopping, that was it; remembering with sharp vividness a little meeting he and I had, the day I accepted Burt.

I was in the bathroom, the door a bit ajar, brushing my teeth when Dad shuffled past on his way to early bed. Mother was out at some church meeting or other. On impulse I pushed the door open wider and called to him.

"Dad?"

"Yes, dear?"

"—you there? Come in a sec." Shyly he put his head

in at the doorway, wrapping the dressing-gown modestly close around the flanks that had engendered me.

"I've had a proposal, Dad, from Burt."

"Have you? And will you accept it, my dear?"

"Yes."

He sat down tentatively on the carefully lowered lid of the toilet. His face was without any discernible expression. Since the heart attack, he had taught himself how to protect and conserve his energy in every way, which meant he could not afford to have deep feelings.

"Well," he said after a brief pause, "I think highly of Burt, and so does your mother. He's stable and reliable; a decent, self-respecting young man. He's sure to be a good husband."

"Yes."

"He's certainly devoted to you, too. I've seen that."

"Yes."

"You're quite—happy about it?" he asked cautiously.

"Oh yes—quite happy—just starting bridal nerves a bit early, maybe."

"Marriage is a very good thing, you know. Your mother and I have found it very good. There's so much strength and comfort in a good partner."

"Oh, yes, Mother's been hinting for years now that it's time I got married. Here I am nearly twenty-six, and that dinosaur Midge got married at twenty—it's really been bothering her."

Mildly, my father allowed this acid-tipped dart to go by without comment.

"Well, it will make a great gap in our lives, my dear; more than you know; but if you're happy, that's what matters most to us."

Suddenly I turned away from the mirror and, glancing swiftly at his gentle head, bent a little in fatigue or sadness, said one of those naked, dangerous things so rarely said between parents and children: "I'll never love any man as much as you." As soon as it was said we were both mildly horrified.

"Dad, you'd better get to bed. You've been up long enough."

"Yes . . . and sleep well yourself, my dear. You've been looking thin and poorly for quite a while; your mother and I have been worried. But now you'll bloom, I expect. 'Like a little rose in a demnition flower pot'."

We smiled, relieved to have smoothed my words over so easily, defused them as it were. Dickens was part of a shared old love, sexless, comfortable, and safe. We said good-night genially and parted.

But it was true, and strange I should have had the prophetic insight to know it so early. I never did love any man as much as I loved my father. Before I married Burt I had already begun in fact to lose the art, or science, of loving anyone. And my father's death fifteen years later only buried that truth, not him.

The shock left me quite trembly, thoughts all disoriented. Looked at first just like a corpse lying there. That awful din on the stairs, and then silence. Hard for me to collect my wits and know what to do, fright is so unfocussing. And I couldn't understand how that door could have been left open.

Well, as I say, had been more than a little absent and vague lately, sleep full of dreams and dragons, not as restful as being awake some nights. One dream, of Dad calling my name, woke me up sweating, and led to a whole long, ugly remembrance of one night when Mother called—one of her several daily calls near the end of his life, to ask for help, reassurance, advice, comfort.

"Again?" Burt asked sourly as I padded back to bed. It was a quarter to twelve.

"She's upset. He won't take his pills."

"She doesn't have to call here. What can *you* do? Let her call the doctor. Fifty times a day—it's a bit much."

I turned over on my side and curled up, trying not to shiver. From Neil's half-opened door came the sound of coughing; he had been home from school all week with bronchitis. If the cough went on—sometimes it tormented him for an hour at a time—I would have to get him a hot drink, poor kid.

Burt put his hand on my thigh, and I moved it away, trying not to be too abrupt. He pulled me back against him, his chest and abdomen still hard and lean, the column of flesh warm between his legs.

"I'm really too tired."

"You're not." His hands grasped my breasts turned hard and insistent, making my nerves flame with irritation.

"No, Burt, please. Let me alone."

"Yes, Burt, please," he said, mocking the whine in my voice.

Grimly I said no more but turned my body to stone. Something about my resistance seemed to enrage him then. He got up and closed the door sharply on Neil's cough. "Now, damn you," he said, and dragged me over on my back. I tried to refuse him, but his anger rose every second to a violent, almost murderous rage. His hands tore at my legs, he bruised my nipples with cruel biting and sucking. Rage gave him more strength than I had; he soon forced my thighs open and entered me with a brutal stab that made me cry out in pain. Furiously, repeatedly, he thrust me, holding me pinned with his weight, his breath sobbing in my ear. He was sweating and trembling at the climax like a man afraid, and in the dark his voice gasping "What about me? What about me?" was the voice of an accuser.

Afterwards he lay apart, face down, on his own side of the bed, and the tearing spasms of his dry tears went on for several minutes. I lay silently, without moving. Neil's muffled coughing still sounded. After a while I got up, stiff and sore, wrapped on a dressing-gown, and went to him.

Burt and I never referred to that episode again, in

words or any other way. But it left a space between us, a cool width never to be bridged. Next day he showed no regret or remorse whatsoever; he only looked colder and tighter than before, with his bloodless lips and pale-blue eyes. As for me, a hard crystal of active dislike never after quite left my tolerance of him. Yet, of course, we went on mechanically together, sharing a roof, a name, a son, and even, at intervals, the ritual of the flesh. When my father died a few months later, I shed no tears at all. I seemed to have forgotten how to feel anything, and what a relief that was. It was what made going on possible. What Burt felt was something else, of course. I guessed it well enough, but it didn't really concern me.

The fall of Adam couldn't have sounded more momentous: a huge din, close enough to shake the air. Just the same, for a few minutes, I thought it had nothing to do with me. Then I thought, "But that was on *my* stairs." And was so startled at the idea of invasion that I went straight out in my nightgown, crossed the furnace area, and looked. There at the foot of the steps lay a sprawled man with a long overcoat fanned out around him. The head was turned; all I could see was curly black hair crowned with a dollar-sized bald spot. On this spot a cut oozed blood. The figure was perfectly still; after the colossal uproar of its fall, the silence seemed to sing. I looked down at the body helplessly. At the top of the stairway, the open door let in a wedge of light and the flat little yellow disc of Mrs. MacNab's face. Characteristically, her first words as she started down the steps were, "Is that *blood*?"

Behind her I glimpsed the two old front-room people and another head or two just arriving, so scuttled away to pull on my coat for decency. When I got back, four or five people were standing gregariously around the fallen man, who still lay there motionless. There was much chat in several languages.

"Don't try to move him."

"Call the police."

"Is he dead or what?"

"Drunk, more like."

"It's that Polack upstairs, isn't it?"

"Who?"

"That one everybody calls Johnny?"

"No, that's not him."

"Yes it is."

"What's he doing down here, anyway?"—suspiciously.

"Better call the police for an ambulance."

Mrs. MacNab, without wasting energy in idle speculation or comment, produced a folded newspaper and put it neatly under the bloody head. Nobody seemed to have a notion what to do next, though there was a good deal of discussion in a babble of French and English, especially from the old couple, who gazed at the spectacle with greedy, gratified eyes, and had a great deal to say.

"He's Czech, not Polish. Lives on the second floor, next to the Leblancs. Cheerful fellow, always has a pleasant word, even if you can't understand much he says. Not the first time he's had a drop too much, of course . . . we often hear him stumbling on the stairs . . . what a terrible thing if he's dead—"

I pressed my fingers to the side of his wrist, and rather to my surprise found a strong, warm pulse beating there.

"He's not dead, only knocked himself out."

"Mr. Horvath," Mrs. MacNab said loudly.

The head moved, the eyelids lifted, and dazed, dark eyes looked vaguely at us all.

"Don't try to get up," I said, pressing him down firmly. "Your back may be hurt."

"Who the hell are you?" he asked in a thick, indignant voice made further opaque by a dense European

76

accent. He gingerly raised a hand to his broken crown, tried to sit up, and then, with dramatic suddenness, vomited copiously over himself and the bottom step.

"Oh Christ," Mrs. MacNab said bitterly.

"Mr. Horvath," said the old lady from the front room, in the gentle voice appropriate to afternoon tea in some ball-fringed parlour, "are you quite all right? I am Mrs. Cooper, can I do anything for you? Mr. Cooper and I met you a few months ago at one of the Dollar Concerts, do you remember, and you lent us a book on Franz Liszt. It was so interesting, too."

"How do you do," said the fallen one with dignity.

A powerful urge to giggle seized me. Before I could restrain him, he sat up, ignoring the vomit, the bloody newspaper, and the spectators with truly superb dignity. If anything, he had the air of one politely ignoring the social lapses of everybody else present.

"Now don't try to stand up till we can tell if you've broken anything," I said. "That was a bad fall. Do you feel all right?"

"Sure," he said. "Fine." He felt his scalp again, vaguely. "These damn stairs too dark, very dangerous."

"Well, don't move for a minute." I fetched a washcloth and cleaned the cut up a little, and then wiped his face for good measure. He looked up at me.

"You are very good woman," he said. "Will you marry me?"

"Now Johnny," Findlay, who had just joined the group, said indulgently.

"I mean it. I love you." He had my hand now in a large, warm grasp. Much amusement in the crowd.

"You're crazy," I said, as kindly as the truth could be put. But my free hand had started to go up automatically to my hair, and that made me grin helplessly.

"Come on now, Johnny," somebody said. "We'll give you a hand up. You're okay now. Heave—ho. Let's go."

Two or three of them hoisted him up and helped him stumble up the stairs, the long skirts of his ex-military overcoat dragging. Mrs. MacNab, tight-mouthed, attacked the mess with a mop and water-bucket, replacing the stink of vomit with an even more repulsive stink of Javex. Everybody reluctantly dispersed; the show was over. The Coopers left last of all.

Well, so much for that, I thought, going back to my own room with alacrity after double-checking to be sure the door above was now locked. I laughed a bit, remembering the absurdity of the whole thing, and then forgot all about it.

January deep-freeze. Still, ice-blue air. Everything static, a glacial arrest. Christmas presumably happened at the usual time; I didn't notice. Zero days, nights of black crystal. In this neighbourhood, where a lot of shift workers lived, there wasn't the same prim barri-cade between night and day, the shops seemed to stay open indifferently, the neon signs blinked colour into the bitter air, the traffic ground away even when the streets were dark and deserted.

Found it convenient to go out mostly late at night or very early, when the first wave of thin light washes over the city. Nobody around then to notice the tennis shoes. Other night-walkers about, bundled and anony-mous, comfortably indifferent to each other, all more or less queer. Occasionally I met a tall woman who wore a kerchief tied over her whole lower face like a train robber, and an old dwarf with a knapsack who sported a child's red tuque. Nobody cared; thank God this was still a civilized city where no questions were asked and walking at night was still legal. Also quite safe. The weasel gangs of teen-agers, the raisin-eyed toughs, the belligerent drunks, all stayed on their own beat—St. Lawrence Main and thereabouts. Per-verts and revolutionaries had their own haunts else-where. The quiet old side streets were left to such odd night-birds as me. Sometimes I walked along for blocks, rubber soles brisk on the squeaking snow, without meeting a soul but a darting cat or two. No eyes to meet but the red and green blink at intersections. Wonderful.

The best hour of all, I discovered, was between five and six, when the grey houses still dreamed in the snow and the hump of the city's old volcano rose slowly out of the dark like an act of creation. It was then you could hear the pure element of silence and see how immense the sky was. In that early fog-frosted light you saw all kinds of things not noticeable later in the day. A bird puffing out its feathers to keep warm. Smoke a dresden-blue plume against the white sky. A puff of frigid air lightly whirling dry snow like sea-spray, just for fun. A massive icicle glittering like a threat. Soon I realized this was the best time, too, for finding things. Nobody around. You could take your time. Amazing what you could pick up. Different times I found a girl's sterling hairclasp, a rosary on a gold chain, a cigarette lighter, a silk head-square from Italy, a man's cane with a silver band initialled "H.T.", and a half-bottle of Scotch planted neck-deep in a snow-bank. I kept most of them for myself, including, of course, the Scotch. The cane was welcome, too, what with all the ice underfoot. Once in a while, though, I'd take a few of the more valuable things along and sell them to a pawnbroker on Craig Street. A dollar or two, I didn't care how little he gave; it came in mighty handy. Once I pulled a big woman's handbag out of a trash basket. Empty, of course. But it was an alligator bag and nearly new. Got five dollars for it.

But I wasn't in the business, not like the real scavengers I saw sometimes, poking in garbage tins; finding things was just a pastime for me. I got just as much fun out of finding things of no value, like the grubby Raggedy Ann doll I rescued from the gutter, or the page I caught on the wind from a kid's exercise book, full of big shaky A's. Things like these kept me in touch, you might say, with the human race, and it was contact without any complications—the most satisfying kind. Couldn't bring myself to throw much of it away. The apartment began to get pretty cluttered. I didn't care.

Sometimes things happened that I found disturbing, though. One night a little boy—he didn't seem more than eight or nine—followed me for blocks and then ran past, gave me a shove, and tried to grab my purse. I hung on; he pulled; we were both frightened. He was panting like a caught bird. Then he ran off down an alley. Silly, but it gave me a bit of a scare, and I avoided that area for a long time. Another night I passed an old house built right on the street corner and just happened to glance up at a lighted window over my head. An old, old man stood there gesticulating. He was shrunk small, with wild grey hair, and his mouth was wide open in a grimace of crazy rage or grief. I turned my head away quickly, but not before he saw me and nodded as if we were old acquaintances. That bothered me more than I can explain. Was he welcoming me to some sort of club? I went straight home and stayed inside for days. Even when I came out again, I took care to avoid that corner, and it was a while before I did any more looking to find things.

When the weather was really frigid, an arctic wind poured down over the frozen cap of the world and petrified everything to iron hardness. Then I stayed indoors and was content there. Secluded and silent. A still point where the globe no longer turned. Nothing to do. No responsibilities. No motives. No plans. Marvellous. Hard to express how peaceful I was inside my own skin. All those inconvenient and often uncomfortable memories that had haunted me in the first months had now, thank God, packed up, and the present was undefiled. I could sit quietly reading for hours or idly thinking, never having any Meaningful Thoughts whatsoever; often, in fact, dozing off in a shamelessly elderly way.

Or in this privacy I could see things. I don't mean just look at, but really see. The gold radius of old tom's one good eye, for instance, as he stared in at me from the window. There was a five-pointed sun at the heart of the pupil, changing as the light changed. (He wanted to come in, the old lush. I wouldn't let him.) Or the plant on the kitchen sill, thriving in the sun, no matter how coldly the blue sky glittered outside. You could look for ever at how the green burned in the delicate tissue of the leaves; see the veins there, functional and also full of grace; trace the exquisite cut line of the leaf edge burning green too in the light. An hour or two could go by while you looked; that is, if you kept track of hours, which I didn't. Why bother? Quite a few things, in fact, seemed to me less and less worth bothering about. Fat rolls of dust idly lolled under the bed. I rarely bothered to make it up or change the sheets. The sink was full of dishes, the bathtub wore a ring. It didn't worry me.

The only thing that did was that door at the top of the cellar stairs. Ever since Adam fell there, I went out three or four times every night to reassure myself that the door at the top was still safely locked. Several times I heard—or thought I heard—someone up there knock or try the knob. But whenever I looked, no one was there. I was perfectly safe. But it did bother me, and I was very, very careful to check the lock often.

It was too good to last, of course, this peaceful, perfect isolation. I forgot to be watchful enough, and late one grey afternoon, in the pawnbroker's to sell a man's watch with a broken strap I'd picked up at a bus-stop, found myself looking straight into Kim's eyes. She was with a boy her own age with an incredible growth of fuzzy blond hair, and they were looking through a rack of scruffy leather jackets.

Quick as a fish I darted out through the debris of Sam's customers, as seedy and used as his goods, and made off down the street. As nimbly as my age would permit, I nipped round the nearest corner. Hurried along, wheezing, didn't dare to glance back or slow down. Pity she'd had time to recognize me—I looked so different now. Just how different, those dark and startled eyes told me plainly enough. Pumped along like a retired track-runner; but then I had to pause; no breath left.

"Gran! Gran—it *is* you." Her breath floated out like a white feather on the grey air. She gripped my arm in a mittened hand to stop me.

"Hi, Kim," I said sheepishly. "Damn it."

"For a minute I wasn't sure . . . why didn't you say hello?"

"Well . . . " weakly. Forced a smile.

"Gran, are you *living* around here?"

"No. Are you?"

She gave a snuffling giggle. "No. Actually, Martin and I came down to buy jackets. Mum won't let me have the cash for a new one, and they're neat, everybody wears them. Look, I told him to take off; I mean, I thought you and I could go somewhere and have coffee or something. How about it?"

"Well . . . "

"Come on, it's cold here."

"There's a little Japanese place up in the next block —just a basement, nothing grand, but they have nice tea."

It was good to sit down in the Oriental fug and gradually my heart stopped rushing around and my wind came back. But Kim across the tiny plastic table seemed all at once to lose her poise. She tipped her long, thick hair down over each side of her face and smoothed it into the obligatory flat, straight locks like blinkers. She cleared her throat, but found nothing to say with it.

I ordered tea and poured it into the little bowls.

Unbundled my head from its scarf, hunched back the torn coat, tucked my feet in the soiled canvas shoes well under the table. Somewhat tentatively I felt for my old identity.

"How's your father, Kim?"

"Oh—you know. Worried. All hung up. I really feel sorry for him. Money and status and three-button suits, that's all he thinks is real."

"Well, so they are, of course."

"You know what I mean. The sad thing is, I think he sometimes wonders, man could I be wrong?—but it's too late for him, I guess."

"Mm. Well, I hope he's not worrying about me. I want you be sure and tell him not to do that. I'm just fine."

"Yes, sure." Kim gave an embarrassed wriggle that almost overturned her tea.

"I really am, you know. Never more so, in fact. The way I look bothers you—but that's not the point. Or maybe it is. Goes with my new lifestyle, you might say."

She grinned uncertainly. "Well, but Gran . . . no kidding, you're so much thinner and everything, for a second I hardly knew you. What's *happened*, anyway? Of course Dad's in a flap about not knowing where you live, or how you get enough to eat, even. Mum is, too, but in a different way. It makes her furious when your friends call up and ask all kinds of questions. She gets even more uptight than Dad about it. She can hack divorce or legal separation, but not what you're doing—it doesn't fit anywhere, and that bugs her."

"I'll bet it does," I said with satisfaction.

"She doesn't like Dad going over so often to see Granddad, either, poor old thing. I went once and he was as mean as an adder. I don't blame you for quitting, actually. Only of course . . . well, he has a house-keeper now, that Dad found out of an agency—she's a

83

million years old and she groans out loud climbing the stairs with his trays."

"I know how she feels."

"But Gran—what are you doing down here? How do you fill up the time—you haven't got a job or anything?"

"No."

"Then you must be—"

"Oh, Kim, I just bumble along. If you're worried about my clothes, don't be. It's all right, really."

Impasse. No way in the world to explain what my life was like now, how private and satisfying. She would never understand about the pleasure of finding things. Close as we were, she would probably never understand that, no matter how long she lived, not after Rosemary's upbringing.

"But you look so poor," blurted Kim. How do you get on, I mean you must need money—"

"Not at all," I said firmly. "I have absolutely everything I need."

"And you don't mind living like this—?"

"I'm happy, Kim."

"Because, honestly, Gran, you . . . you don't look it."

That made me flinch, all right. "Don't look it! Just because I've got a bit shabby, is that what you mean?"

"No, it's not, not at all. Like, here I am buying a beat-up old leather jacket to wear because that's what I like . . . my mother says I can't bring it into the house, even, in case it's dirty or has bugs. I'll have to keep it at Martin's. No, it's not that, I just mean you look . . . so different . . . like much older . . . or something—"

Her voice trailed off diffidently. I was thankful, for once, that like all her generation she was inept with words. as if they were an alien form of expression. But I'd forgotten the ruthless honesty behind this fractured syntax and vocabulary.

"Like. Gran, aren't you wondering now sort of who you are?"

84

"Like no," I said coldly.

She smoothed down her side hair again in two nervous hands. Her face had gone perfectly blank. At once I felt ashamed.

"Well, let me try to explain. It's true that now I'm neither wife, maid, nor mother. But I'm myself, for the first time, nearly, since I was a teen-ager like you." I poured the last of the tea into her bowl and pushed it toward her. "Look, I'll tell you something about me and my mother, Kim. I always felt a bit scornful of her, because she was so desperately conventional. When my brother, Oliver, joined up in 1916—he was just turned eighteen—she was proud, because it was patriotic of him, it was the Right Thing to do. You belong to the first generation to know for sure that wars are stupid. Mine was beginning to suspect it, but not in time, and we didn't say it out loud. My mother's honestly didn't know. Not till afterward. But when Oliver was killed, less than a year later, she had to face it. She knew then that nearly everything she once believed in was a lie, and she had to decide whether to reject it or pretend it was still true, all that about gallantry and honour. . . . "

"Which did she?"

"The brave thing. Pretended it was still true. And I didn't have the wisdom to love her for that. Not till now."

Kim nodded. Her eyes, with their startled, dreamy look, were calm. I relaxed a little.

"Now I've chosen the other way, you see. Rejected everything I was brought up to value. It looks completely selfish, and it is. But it's right for me. It's easy, really. You just give up your pride. Anyhow, I've chosen this and I'm going to stay with it now. Right to the end."

Kim cleared her throat again. "Yeah. Well . . . " she shifted and tossed back some of the hair. "Look it's dark. I'd better take off. Gran, I wish I could see you again. I mean, it's been nice talking to you."

"Yes. Well, perhaps we'll run into each other again some time. I occasionally go into Sam's . . . to look around."

"Wait—I'm paying for the tea, Gran."

"No, you're not. I am not on welfare, dear."

"But I mean it. Put that away."

"Kim, don't be silly—"

But her hard, surprisingly strong, little hand shoved mine away, and she paid the bill and marched me out, triumphant. We stood outside for a few minutes in the lazily falling snow, awkward and painfully polite.

"It was awfully nice to see you, Kim."

"Take care, now, Gran."

"Be sure to tell your father I'm fine. I'll give him a call one of these days."

"Yeah. He'd like to hear from you."

"So long, then, dear."

"'Bye now."

When she was well out of sight, I hitched up my coat-collar and began to plough slowly home. Felt extremely tired; unnaturally, profoundly tired. When I got back at last and had my door safely locked. I took off all my clothes and went straight to bed. And there a black depression folded itself over me, a defeat as total, as heavy, as death itself.

Before long, I knew this was an illness. Not like the one before. There were no physical symptoms this time to comfort me—then you have something to get hold of. We're all unqualified doctors these days from watching TV, specialists if we read the "Medicine" section of *Time*. No, this was something different and worse than a virus. I just stayed in bed. Hoped it might go away, this leaden, nameless misery. It didn't. Once I thought in panic, "I must make an effort," and began to get dressed. But the feel of my soggy old bra and the sight of a spongy run in one stocking were enough to make me drop the clothes back on the floor and climb into bed again.

It wasn't so bad when sleep came, but it rarely did. Most of the time I just drifted on a scummy sea of half-thoughts and memories, all of them obscene and ugly, full of pain. The time a man living on our street invited seven-year-old me in for candy and fondled the front of my middy blouse with blind fingers, his eyes blank with a shamed suffering there is no name for, while his mouth made bright chat to divert my attention. In spite of this, the touching gave me a queer, uneasy pleasure. I never told anyone. The time I saw a milkman climb down from his wagon on purpose to kick his horse in the belly. The fat Jewish girl in our Grade Eight class with the oily hair and oily skin and a name so unpronounceable we could only repeat it with strangled giggling . . . the teacher, a spectacled, tight girl from Calgary, who smelled of Noxzema and sang in the choir, liked to be sarcastic to Roslyn. "Would it be asking too much . . . ?" she would say. "We aren't taking up too much of your time, are we?" The class squirmed with joy, and so did I, but I loathed that woman just the same. How I hated her. My brother coming home early one New Year's Eve from a party and sobbing on his bed, a big, handsome boy of eighteen, because some girl had treated him badly. A dog I once heard screaming for half an hour after a truck hit it. My mother's lifted, tight-mouthed, ruined face confronting the world in silence after Oliver's death. Burt's tormented breathing the night he raped me.

And when not turning over such charming souvenirs of the past, I lay immersed in present time like someone helpless, buried up to the chin in shit. The window over my head was bleared with dirty snow. A tap dripped in the kitchen, where a sour stink presided over crusty dishes and pots. The old tomcat outside screamed like a soul in torment. The wind blew, a desolate sound that went on and on.

At intervals I shuffled to the bathroom or made a cup of tea. But I didn't get dressed. Lost touch with reasons to do anything at all. My hair snarled hopelessly. I couldn't be bothered to comb it. The soles of my feet grew black from padding barefoot here and there. Grit and dust gathered in the bed. Sometimes I wept, but not often, because all that did was leave me with scalded eyes and a head swollen with pain.

The plant in the kitchen window shrivelled and turned brown. Sourly, obsessively, I made lists of people to blame. My mother. Burt. Above all, Kim. What a disaster, running into that kid; why did it have to happen when I was getting on so well? Her polite, incredulous eyes looking at my coat—I couldn't forget them.

Why had I been fool enough to try to explain myself to her? It was like asking and being refused. She had undermined me now hopelessly. Ignorant, arrogant little bitch, what right had anyone that age to challenge me like that? How did the young come by their appalling self-righteousness, anyhow, their awful self-confidence, their destructive, cool contempt? What kind of a terrible world would they build with such tools? Kim would find another way to be as essentially frigid and phony as her mother. To think now of how sentimentally I used to love her made me squirm.

My fingernails grew and broke off raggedly. My breath grew sour. The wind blew and blew.

Then the dreams. Crazy, nightmare fantasies full of grotesque shapes of fear. Running with bloody hands. Battering and beating to death Miss Rogers, who turned out to be Roslyn, on her back groaning and panting in sexual orgasm. A long ribbon of bowel dragged out of a living animal, Pat's smiling mouth open to reveal a huge phallus for tongue . . . knocking, shrieks, running and falling with a huge drop, waking with a great jerk and moan to hear the wind

88

still blowing. Then sleep again without intermission, running again, battering a locked door barehanded in agony to escape, bang, bang, bang, my father whimpering as I pushed him over, bang, bang, a cat running after me in the dark, vicious and predatory, while I tried to escape, rattling the locked door in a frenzy—

Out. Get out. Get up and run. Stone legs dragging. Bang, bang. Dark, fusty, run, crawl. bang, the stairs, head light as a bubble. Fumble with the lock. Open the door. Light, a shock like birth.

"Mrs.? You been sick, I never see you out for nine, ten days? You take this little gift. I intrude, I make a mess your stairs. I try apologize, often knock, you never come. But you take this. I wish you well."

I gaped at him stupidly. The drunk in the long overcoat, the Czech upstairs. Holding out a paper bag and a hopeful smile. "You so sick, poor lady. I can help you at all?"

"No, thank you."

He made a little bow and tactfully disappeared. I closed and locked the door. Groped slowly back downstairs, a bit giddy, bare feet tentative on the cold cement floor.

Opened the bag. A dark bottle of wine. Wrestled out the cork, a long struggle that made me sweat, and took a large swallow without the formality of a glass. Stomach received this surprise with consternation, but after a brief uncertainty decided to accept it. A pleasant warmth spread. A taste like wet fur. Another swallow and things cleared. Blood started sluggishly to move about its business. I sat down on the dishevelled bed and tilted the bottle again.

Noticed a few minutes later, with a frown of surprise and disapproval, the filth of my bare feet and the stains on my crumpled nightgown. Put a hand up to my dry tangle of hair and tried to smooth it out. Another swig.

Then I padded along to the bathroom and turned

on both taps full blast, dragging the nightgown off as I waited. My tongue tasted like a goat's. I squeezed out toothpaste inefficiently and scrubbed my teeth hard. Naked as the newborn, weak and shivery, I stepped into the bath-water and washed myself clean. The effort was exhausting, my head spun with weakness, and afterwards all I could do was flop helplessly back into bed. But when I slept there were no more nightmares.

As soon as my strength came back, I set out to room-hunt. Two reasons: it would be prudent to avoid any possibility of meeting Kim again, and several times in the days following the Czech's visit there was a knocking at my door . . . he was obviously going to be a nuisance. So one pale-blue morning I set out with the classified ads under one arm to look at a place in Montreal North—"a large room with balcony overlooking garden". Still felt a bit wavery and uncertain on my legs, but that black depression had lifted. Still air outside smelled of damp biscuits, weak sun in a wide sky beamed vacantly like an infant's smile. Nice to be on the bus, riding along with a dreamy lurch and swing, past miles of shops, schools, houses with twisted outside stairs. Bus nearly empty; driver whistling. Chicken feathers sailing cheerfully down St. Lawrence Main where the kosher butchers did their thing.

Yes, a garden would be a nice change, so would a balcony, after these months of moledom. Living in a cellar was bad for the morale, after all; too much like being buried.

The house, when I finally located it, turned out to be a mock fort with crenellations and a watch-tower; I almost expected a drawbridge to rattle down when I rang the doorbell. A char-woman in a blue apron let me in, and I stepped at once up to the eyebrows in darkness and a smell of dog. Somewhere near by, a radio was blatting out a waltz. The char disappeared to find "Madame", and I was left alone, peering about to discover the source of a desperate scratching and scuffling somewhere near my feet. Gradually I made out the form of an elderly Scottie who seemed to be wearing a white shirt and shorts. A minute later I could see his outfit was made of a man's long-underwear leg.

"He has eczema," explained Madame, when she finally materialized. Very old, deaf as a cloud, and so enormously, softly fat that only layers of buttoned sweaters and what seemed to be two or three dresses on top of each other held the billows of her flesh together. She moved with the vague dignity and inefficiency of a captive balloon. The waltz ended with a thump. She and the dog wheezed together on six or seven notes as we all climbed the stairs. "You have just heard the Robin Hood Chorchestra and Orus—" announced the radio. On the landing our way was lighted by an elaborate ceiling-lamp, five pimpled green glass udders hanging from a long chain.

Someone mercy-killed the announcer and in the silence could be heard a rapid series of shrill little farts as Madame groped along the hall ahead of me. "Monsieur Lemieux used to 'ave this room," she panted, "until he die, that is, nothing catching you understand, it was the stones, I have a touch of it myself, but when the pain gets bad, you just take a cup of gin. A beautiful room, very tasty."

The room was cavernous and the sagging double bed looked as if the late occupant might very well still be in it. Madame wallowed across the floor, still issuing an occasional high-pitched remark from the other end, and wrestled open a pair of tall French doors to display the balcony, a narrow, ornamental gangway containing much snow and a perfectly incredible collection of pigeon droppings.

"Lovely, eh?" she asked proudly. She then swam over to the window to lift the lace curtain and show the garden. I stared as hard as possible at the big wardrobe with its brass handles, because another series of farts had broken out like sporadic gunfire as soon as she began to eulogize the garden. When I did peer down at it dutifully, all that could be seen was one bush and a garbage tin, overlooked by a large establishment with a huge neon sign: "Salons funéraires".

I fumbled a handkerchief out of my purse and coughed into it vigorously for some time.

"Well, it's very nice, but . . . perhaps you could let me think it over—I could call you at noon, maybe?"

"Oh, certainly," said Madame amiably. She closed the door behind us with care, not to disturb the late occupant. As we made our way back along the hall, there was a prolonged flushing noise behind the bath-room door. This was followed by a loud thump and a muffled shout. Madame shuffled serenely on without pausing. Halfway down the stairs we met the char coming violently up.

"Didn't you hear that?" she demanded. "It's the Colonel, God damn it; he's fallen into the bathtub again."

Desperate by now, I got myself out of there with all speed, and once outside, trotted fast to the nearest corner, rounded it, leaned against a post office, and had a seizure of hysterics. I laughed till it hurt to breathe. Tears poured down my face. I couldn't stop for ages, even though all that wheezing and gasping made shoppers gawk. I wiped my eyes and tried to sober up, but fresh paroxysms kept seizing me. Even when I was able finally to make for the bus-stop, a crazy grin kept pulling my mouth crooked.

Well, perhaps the old basement would do till spring after all. Because life with the Colonel and the Scottie in underwear under those green glass udders would finish me in no time, and I would join M. Lemieux in Abraham's bosom. Meanwhile, I would stop off at a supermarket on the way home and buy a cheap little plant.

Why Harry, of all people, should have come into my head the next day I can't say, but he arrived with the Czechoslovakian's knock and stayed and stayed, though I hadn't given him a thought in probably thirty years. "Drat that fellow," I thought, waiting for the Czech to go away. But Harry's face came in instead, with its curly, fair hair, its broken nose and wrinkled forehead that gave him the look of a worried baby.

It was May's arthritic old car that introduced us. The thing broke down just as the two of us were setting out for a week-end holiday, and we limped it into the nearest garage, a body-shop called Harry's Place. He bent his curly head over the Chev's confused anatomy, and after a few minutes of concentration looked up with a flash of white teeth in his dirty face to say cheerfully, "Lady, if I was you, I think I'd shoot it." However, once he understood the situation, he got to work on it, to the total neglect of his other customers. For three oily hours he clanked away, stopping only once, to send his overalled boy out for coffee all round.

After that, May always took the car to him, though his place was inconvenient to get at, because, besides being a good mechanic, he was so agreeable and helpful. With his shy, cheerful grin and his trusty spanner, he kept that old Chev alive single-handed for another six months. Then, when my Uncle Chester died and left me three hundred dollars, I made up my mind to buy a second-hand car, and Harry spent hours with me shopping around the lots for a good one. When we finally drove away with an elderly Willys, he was as high with delight as a child, though his own business was floundering, and May had told me he had wife trouble as well. He never said a word to me about either of these problems, though.

"Once I get a new fuel pump in," Harry said, "you got yourself a honey of a car here."

"There's just one little detail bothering me . . . I've only been behind a wheel a few times in the country with May right there, and the truth is, I'm scared to death now I have this thing."

Harry laughed and wiped off the steering-wheel carefully with a bit of waste. "Is that all that's botherin' you? I'll teach you to drive, make you an expert in two weeks if you like. This place is folding up, I'll be on relief anyway; lots of time on my hands."

"Well, but look—" I said dubiously, "you'd have to let me pay you—"

"I wouldn't take nothing from you," he said quickly. "Want to start tomorrow? Days are getting longer now; I could pick you up any time after six-thirty."

So, evening after spring evening, Harry taught me to drive. He would call at the house on the dot of seven, his curly hair combed wet, his square hands and golden forearms scrubbed immaculately clean, and always a clean shirt on, its folds crisp from the laundry.

"I don't know why you want to drive a car," my mother said uneasily. "A lady hardly needs to do that sort of thing, do you think? A young girl like you?"

But we took her out with us several times and something about Harry—his jokes or his curly hair—disarmed her and made her cheeks pinken up like a girl's. He took to bringing along boxes of drugstore candy, which he would leave for us shyly, without a word, under the straight chair in the hall. He seemed to have no family of his own and never mentioned his wife.

One evening the corrugations in his forehead were deeper than usual, and he had a piece of stiff paper in his shirt pocket. After we'd practised turning, backing, and stopping on hills, he said "Will you come with me somewhere for coffee? Want to ask you . . .

show you this thing. It ain't a summons—I don't know just what it is."

It was an eviction notice. Unless he got all his belongings out of his de Gaspé Street flat by the next day they would be seized for non-payment of rent, and a bailiff would be on the premises to move him out.

"Well, you'll have to act pretty fast—how long have you had this?—you've only got till tomorrow to find the back rent. Is there much furniture? Maybe you could get hold of somebody you know that has a truck and would keep it for you for a few days . . . ?"

"No, my wife took nearly everything when she left with the kid. There's only some clothes and a radio and like that. But I won't get out—why should I? It's my place, I got a lease, and that rent was paid on the dot every time, till just this last month, it makes me sore that bas— that landlord guy doin' this, he's even full of mean talk about attachin' my stuff at the shop. Well. I'll show him. I'll make it as tough for him as I can. They'll have to drag me out of that flat, let them call the cops, I don't care no more."

He lit a cigarette and tried to hunch his anxious baby face into a smile.

"But Harry—"

"Anyhow, if they do shove me in jail, you can park on a dime now. Don't need the teacher no more."

"Look, Harry, we'll go straight along there now and pack up your things. Fix up with a friend who'll give you a bed for a few nights. I'll help you with the stuff in the flat, we can put it in our basement at home till you . . . settle somewhere."

He put up a stubborn defence against all these suggestions, but at last agreed. I phoned home, and we drove to the flat through a twilight delicate with tender new leaves. The flat was the top layer of a triplex, with rickety steps curling up steeply to a set of cheap, small rooms with thickly varnished floors. There wasn't much to be packed up, though he had some rather handsome leather luggage, and a surprising amount of up-to-date kitchen equipment—such as a glittering chrome toaster—all for some reason left behind by the wife. A vase holding dusty yellow paper roses sat on the dirty kitchen table. There was a brand-new and expensive child-sized car with pedals and steering, inexplicably left in one empty bedroom. "My kid's," he said. "I guess my wife couldn't get it down the stairs. She took about everything else that would lift. He was four in March. I got him that for his birthday. Smart little kid, you should of seen him riding it. Parks as good as you do."

The empty rooms with their silt of boxes, loose newspapers, filled ashtrays, depressed me more than they seemed to bother him. On the kitchen floor I found a creased snapshot of a dour old man in a bowler, cockily smoking a long cigar, and he said quite cheerfully, "That was my Dad. Died with cancer last year. Only weighed seventy pounds at the end. Well, I couldn't help feelin' sorry for the old sod, but he sure gave us all a bad time at home. Used to hit my mother, and when I got old enough to step up to him, he'd belt me too. Broke my nose for me once. Soon as I got old enough, he had me shoved into that Boys' Farm up north, which ain't a nice thing to do to your son either. Just the same, I went to see him in the hospital a few times, none of the rest would go, but the poor old bu—geezer, he had a pretty bad time before the end."

"What a nice man you are, Harry."

His blue eyes rested on me for a moment, but he said nothing more. When we had made the last of a dozen trips up and down the stairs and packed all his things into the car trunk, he switched off all the glaring overhead bulbs, and a gentle April dusk came to the windows and looked in at the silent rooms. Harry took my hands in his two hard ones and pressed them for a second against the clean shirt. The warmth of his healthy flesh came through, and he turned away at once.

"We'd better get along," he said. "This ain't a place for you. Your mother'll be wondering. Will you drive, or you want me to?"

About a week later, after a lesson in what Harry called "mergin' with traffic", he told me I was ready to apply for a license. "Nothin' to it," he said. "They don't ask questions or take you out for a test drive or nothin', not like in the States or Ontario. But I didn't tell you that before, I wanted to be sure you could take care of yourself okay in the car before you got your license. But you're fine, goin' to be a real good driver."

"If I am, it's because you're a good teacher."

"Why don't we leave the car here and walk in the park for a bit: Lafontaine Park, you know it?—they got swans over there in the pond. It's still quite light."

So we parked the car and strolled into the park— how funny, it's so near where I live now—just drifted along the paths under a sky pearling slowly with an early moonrise. It was chilly for May, and there were only a few rapt, interlaced couples on the benches. Harry took my hand as we ambled slowly along. The sky greened. A star or two showed. Then the moon lifted over the dark trees. The pond, spanned by a little rustic bridge, showed only as a glimmer in the dusk. We leaned on the bridge railing for a while, waiting for the swans.

"You'll be goin' away this summer, I guess," he said.

"Yes, some cousins have asked us to their place in the Maritimes. Dull but healthy."

"Might take a trip to Maine myself . . . take the kid. Maybe even talk the wife into comin' along."

"That would be nice."

"Yeah. I'd like to give Johnny a good time. He's a nice little kid."

"I hope everything works out well for you, Harry."

"You too. I hope you like your new school." For that was the year I transferred from the grimy brick east-end school with its pale, undernourished kids and vicious bullying and humiliating monthly visits from a city nurse who grimly searched their heads for lice. Armed with my new M.A., I went that fall to the midtown high school where Patrick Devlin was principal, which gave Harry's good wishes a post-operative irony neither of us recognized, of course, at the time. What preoccupied us just then was the current of physical pleasure and affection so warmly and naturally flowing between our clasped hands—a silent, powerful bond just pleasantly tinged with sadness, because there was nothing in the world that could be done about it.

No swans appeared, though we lingered till the moon was high and bright as a dime. We hung over the rail, listening as if bemused to the gentle lap of the water. It would be our last evening together; we both knew that and accepted it without protest. But we had something to give each other, and gave it in silence as we watched for the swans—Harry, in the loneliness of his lost marriage, touching the loneliness of my pedantic, inhibited, celibate young life. We lingered there a long time, our hands clasped, but no swans appeared. Probably there never were any there. At last, when the moon was high and small we walked slowly out of the park, saying nothing. We parted casually, but avoided the word "good-bye".

I only saw Harry once or twice after that, and never alone. He moved away, I think, to some other city. I never thought of him again, really, in all this time, until that crazy Czech's knocking for some reason brought him so vividly to mind that I could remember the precise shade of bird's-egg blue in his eyes under that worried baby's forehead.

Yes, Harry's undeveloped attraction was the beginning, really, of what ended for me in my fifties, when, to my consternation, a few stiff grey hairs appeared on my chin, and men looked at, but no longer saw, me.

Never did get quite used to that—being neutered is pretty dreary. Something so basic about being desired; much simpler and easier than being loved, and maybe more necessary to a woman's mental health. I pondered the whole business a lot on my finding expeditions early in the bleached February mornings.

Not that having the sexual charge was all that idyllic at the time. Led, in fact, to all sorts of the most awkward embarrassments and impasses. Furthermore, there were times in my life when nobody, absolutely nobody, found me attractive. Through most of my girlhood I was so tight with egotism and intelligence that I might have been bodiless as far as boys could tell. You can't count sad freaks like the blouse-feeler, of course; the really poignant fact is, I wasn't kissed till I was eighteen, and then it was only by a theology student with damp hands like a frog. For ages only the most wildly unsuitable people pursued me— psychologically retarded men of all ages with nothing in common but their unattractiveness. That neurotic boy at Macdonald, for instance, in the Philosophy of Education course: at twenty he'd already had two nervous breakdowns because he felt guilty about hating his mother. Or the janitor at the slum school who used to eye me boldly and one day sidled up and tried to feel my bottom. Or perhaps the best of the collection, the canon of seventy who used to visit Dad with sherry and religious consolation, and tickled my palm with his dry, warm, wicked old finger. Men like these often plunged me into dark brooding in those days. May, for instance, was always being courted by attractive, *normal* kinds of males. It wasn't fair. I had a skin like porcelain and lots of glossy, golden-brown hair, well-shaped if rather ample hips; why was it only the pimply ones, compulsive coughers, vegetarians, and communists who asked me for dates?

Still, they did ask. And the interlude with Pat, for all its dire pangs, did happen. So did life with Burt, even if they both confirmed my suspicion that sex was a detail I had better learn to consider trivial. (May, in the meantime, had moved to New York, and was going comfortably to bed twice a week with a book salesman who had a wife in Albany. That lasted twenty serene years, while Burt and I snarled and snapped in a marriage that had turned into a cage.)

An umbrella—charming orange, yellow, and green flowers in silk, and only one broken spoke. Looks like spring. Take it along.

No doubt about it, though: dealing in general with the male population—customs men, doctors, electricians, taxi-drivers—a woman gets used to a certain kind of attention. When that stops, you feel surprised and a bit depressed. It's disconcerting to get the same blank waiter's solicitude from them all, specially if, like me, even your husband no longer finds you interesting, bodily or personally.

Not that, God knows, I wanted any change in that now. If ever a drunk swaying home in the small hours, or a late, lonely street-prowler paused to glance at me speculatively, I hurried along in a nervous fluster till I shook them off. It was ludicrous to think, for instance, that the persistence of that crazy Czech meant . . . and crazier to be tempted even for a second to let him in, even on nights when the silence of my rooms in the basement got thick enough to cut into blocks like earth. No, it was sweetly peaceful to be finished with all that.

Only, whenever I saw a bus-driver eyeing a woman's long legs as she climbed the high step, or a boy with his arm locked around a long-haired, laughing girl, I felt a sort of fierce irritation that made me turn away my eyes.

One Monday morning I found a confused but complete *New York Times* on top of a trash basket, and took it home in a thick wad under my arm to read later. A long time since I'd read a newspaper, and I

100

never listened to the news broadcasts. Why upset yourself; the world isn't likely to get up to anything very new, I thought. If it would just let me alone I'd be glad to return the compliment. But the *Times* had a great many attractions quite apart from politics, wars, and stock markets. The huge ads for women's smart clothes were something to gaze at without jealousy or desire. And the social pages were always absorbing—the vanity of human wishes illustrated by a picture of Miss Gertrude Belch smirking in her wedding veil. Or the enigmatic miracle of the human condition summed up under *Births:* "Hi! I'm Staci Mae Harukomo and I weigh five pounds. Mommy fine, Daddy recovering." Or those memorial verses the fortunate dead could not read. And I profoundly enjoyed the smaller news items, little parables of human absurdity. SOUTH AFRICAN OFFICIAL POLICY: JAPANESE DECLARED HONORARY WHITES. FISTFIGHT AT FEMINIST PEACE MEETING. You could read how the spacemen left their urine in little bags on the moon; or how Princess Margaret's husband was reported to have said to her in public, "God, how you bore me." When that palled, if it ever did, you could turn to the book-review section for higher things.

The lead article was a vastly erudite essay all about rivers and literature. "The seminal image of water," the learned author pointed out, "flows through the literary culture of every major country, beginning with the earliest known Egyptian narrative which was constructed around the archetypal Nile and its gods. Water as a symbol of the viable continuity, the magic and mystery of life, runs through . . . " I was deep in all this when a faint, almost shy sound made me glance down. With blank dismay I saw that a slow but purposeful worm of water was making its way across the floor.

Hastily I cast aside the rustling heaps of newsprint and got up to track the water to its source. Discovered the bathroom floor was inches deep and the toilet was muttering to itself in a plaintive sort of way. Damn. Also blast. Late as it was—close to midnight—I would have to get some clothes on and rouse Findlay.

But when I knocked and knocked again at the door leading to the back rooms shared by the MacNabs, nobody responded at all. After a while, a tousled head of curls appeared over the banister above, and a voice hissed, "Is nobody there, Mrs. Poor Findlay taken to hospital today with his heart, very bad trouble, his mother with him; did you not know?"

"No, I didn't. Well, there's a bad leak in the basement plumbing. It can't wait till morning—I'll drown."

"Not worry. I come," the voice promised.

A moment later, the Czech came rapidly down the basement stairs, the long military coat flung on over cerise pyjamas exuberant with polka-dots. He clucked with high disapproval at the water, now washing in a gentle tide across the central hall to our very feet.

"A flashlight, get. So I can find the watercock. This light no good. Where is your flashlight, Mrs.?"

"I haven't got one."

"Tut!" he said, and frowned with such severity I felt quite crushed and asked meekly, "Wouldn't matches do?"

"Yes, yes, get matches—"

After standing about on the kitchen chair in various unlikely corners of the furnace room, he at last located the cock, but it was stiff, and he had to hit it repeatedly with a number of unsuitable weapons like the orange silk umbrella before it would turn.

"Why have you no wrench?" he grumbled. "Everybody need a wrench sometimes, even a lady like you. How you expect to fix anything with parasols and canes?"

"Sorry," I said, with injured irony.

At last he was able to shut off the water, but by that time I stood in water up to the ankles, and the sitting room floor was awash around a sodden heap of the *Times*.

"We call first thing tomorrow the plumber," he said, nodding grimly at the water as if to keep it in order by threats. "Now I help you mop this—you have a mop, Mrs., I suppose? And pail? Give me."

Without much protest I let him begin sopping up the worst of the mess. My feet ached with cold, and after a while, observing that he was wet almost to his polka-dot knees, I went to the kitchen and made cocoa.

It took hours to blot up all that water. It had contrived to spread and soak an incredible number of my things. Until he began to shift and dry it all up I hadn't realized how many things I seemed to have accumulated—things I'd found and, for one reason or another, kept.

"You quite a collector," the Czech remarked genially. "I like that. Things can be friends, mean something. I never agree with Goethe when he say *'die grösse Kunst, sich zu beschränken und zu isolieren—'*"

"What's that?"

"He says the art best of all is to limit yourself and isolate, be alone—"

"Then he's right." It tickled me to hear Goethe quoted in my basement by a barefoot refugee in pyjamas.

"No, he is wrong. Have lots of things near and be close to someone, that is art, the art of life. You know that or you not have all these things. Books too. I have hundreds of books, have to keep some under the bed; you borrow whenever you like."

The cocoa, of which he had by now had two large mugs, seemed to have given him the energy to be both philosophical and practical. He worked steadily on and on, lifting furniture, mopping and wringing, though I offered several times to take over. But not till the place was relatively dry did he stop.

"You've been very kind," I said.

He wrung out the mop for the last time before twisting a last slop of water out of the hem of his coat. Then he grinned, showing a broken front tooth that gave his smile a six-year-old, rather appealing ugliness.

"I owe you a clean. Well, that look better now, eh? And now you know something? I'm hungry as two wolves."

"Are you? Well, I'm afraid I haven't got much on hand just now—a tin of soup, maybe? I'm not a great eater myself any more . . . "

"Tins of soup!" he said with scorn. "No, no. You wait right here, Mrs. I have eggs." And with that he bolted up the stairs, his long overcoat flying. A moment later he was back, cradling a half-dozen eggs, some seeded rye bread, a box of mushrooms, a jar of paprika, and a bottle of red wine.

"Now we eat," he announced and led the way briskly to my kitchen. "Two eggs or three?" he demanded, pausing only a second as he cracked them into the sizzling butter.

'Oh, I don't think—one, maybe."

"Silly. You have two. I am very good cook, you know. This a fine stove. I have just one hot plate upstairs and no frig, have to use the window-sill, but I love to eat, love to cook. Now, you like a little mushroom? Butter the bread, then, and open the wine— you have a corkscrew? We celebrate that you not drown."

Mildly amused, I set out plates and forks, and found a couple of tumblers for the wine. A rather agreeable smell of fried eggs filled the kitchen. He flipped them over expertly in the pan, whistling as he dusted on salt and pepper, a superbly ridiculous figure in the cerise pyjamas and long overcoat. The overhead light bounced off the bald spot of his crown. With a flourish he filled our plates and served the wine—a good Beaujolais I was surprised to see—and by the time we sat down, our knees almost touching under the tiny kitchen table, I was really quite hungry.

"Good, eh?" he demanded.

"Yes, very good."

"Better than a lousy tin of soup."

"Yes, much better."

"Modest bugger, aren't you?" I thought, but the hot eggs were surprisingly good, and I had no trouble disposing of two. "Eat, eat," he urged me. "Canadians don't know how to eat. They afraid of good food—afraid of all pleasure. Terrible country. Terrible shy people. *Prosit.*"

"Now hold on a minute," I said. But he went on exuberantly. "Too cold wintertimes, it chills their blood and makes puritans." He tipped down his wine with a wink so mischievous it was impossible to find him as irritating as I suspected he really was.

"What country are you from, then?" I asked. Not that I really cared, but one had to say something over a meal.

"I am from Hungarian mother, Czech father, lived in Hungary. In 1956 when was the revolt I come here. The Soviets caught me first. I was important dispatch-rider with my motorcycle for Nagy. They put me in prison four weeks. With chains, Mrs. In Canada, no-body really believe yet that a man can still be prisoner with chains. Then I got out, long story how, I have friends, cousins, they hide me each one a different night . . . did not dare go home, of course. I had to get out, leave without good-bye to my wife and two sons. Have not seen them now for twelve years. One son is married now. Cannot get my wife out of the country. They tell her not to apply for passport, she is afraid now even to ask."

"What a pity. You must have found it very hard to settle down here—learn a new language and everything."

"Oh, not so bad. Before I speak German and French, then I learn English. Speak it now quite well. Canada

105

is too cold winters, but I like here, you can have a good life. Found a good job in a factory making schoolbags, suitcases, things like that. On the machines you can make quite well, even money enough to get drunk sometimes, get woman sometimes, eat well. . . . " He smiled at me broadly. "Yes, I cook lovely meals. Beef stroganoff, goulash, chicken paprika. Delicious!"

"Sounds very nice," I said politely.

"This house good place to live, too. Nobody interfere with you. I like singing, nobody ever complain."

Holding in a yawn, I murmured that that was nice, too. The wine was pleasant, I felt warm and sleepy and wished he would go. But he did not, until the bottle had been tilted to its last drain, and he had stacked up the dishes neatly, talking all the time.

"Yes, except for the Pope Quebec a good place to live, and even the French catch onto him by now, they soon throw the Church out altogether like in France, and a good thing too. . . . "

"No doubt."

"Only good thing the Church does is send police to raid these places that sell all the dirty books, you never see such filthy magazines and pictures, no wonder young girls and boys all mixed up, should all be burned, these newspaper places, like rat nests, more dangerous than that. . . . "

"Yes, I'm sure."

"And the money pouring out for such filth, you can't believe it, and with inflation turning our good money to paper, I don't know what that professor in Ottawa, that Trudeau, what he think, he better get his head out of the library, this country in trouble, I think we having the start of a big depression. But if he had the brave to put price- and wage-control, we could stop inflation, only he can't because big business too strong here. . . . "

"I daresay." This time I let the yawn escape.

At last, then, he hitched together the long overcoat

106

and, taking my hand, lifted and kissed it with warm, moist lips and a most courtly bow.

"You are a very charming lady," he said. "You maybe come and see my place upstairs some day, I cook you a real Hungarian meal." His warm, dark eyes rested on me till I began to feel a trifle self-conscious.

"Thanks for your help tonight," I said, extricating my hand. "It was really good of you—I don't know what I'd have done . . . " And with a murmur of such courtesies, I escorted him to the stairs. There we were delayed further while he developed a series of vigorous views on Mayor Drapeau; but finally he said good-night, and I was able to lock the door on him. Wearily I plodded back to my domain and crawled, yawning horribly, into bed. The whole place smelled of fried eggs.

In the morning I woke twinging all over with rheumatic protests against all that chill and dampness, and, rather unfairly, felt no more indulgent amusement toward the Hungarian. It would be intolerable if he took to coming confidently around, as he no doubt would after the cosy little supper I'd been fool enough to share with him. He had all the earmarks of a Grade A, three-star bore. It made me crosser than ever to remember how pleasant I'd been to him.

While the plumbers did their clanking job that afternoon in my bathroom, went out and spent hours walking rather aimlessly, not looking for things ("You quite a collector"), but just keeping clear of the house till quite late, in case he thought of calling in. What an infernal nuisance. It was a double irritation—first, to be under an obligation to the man, and second, to feel sheepish about avoiding him. When I came home, I peered furtively into the main hall and up the main staircase before nipping in, and with as little sound as possible bolted down the basement stairs to my burrow. All the rest of that night I was edgy, waiting for a knock. The next day was nearly as bad—worse, in fact, because a sleet storm kept me in all through my best finding hours, and I had nothing to do but be bored and have the fidgets.

It struck me the house was unusually quiet. There was a sense of waiting in it. No scrape of Findlay's shovel, no clank of his mother's eternal pail; it occurred to me to wonder if he was better, and with fleeting pity, what she would ever do if he wasn't.

Next day was bright, watery with sun and a washed blue sky. No calls from the Hungarian. I began to relax a little. Perhaps he had too many interests to be a real nuisance after all. Morbid of me to get it into my head that he . . . no; of course not. Met Mrs. MacNab in the hall, just in from the hospital, and for a second hardly knew her. A line of lipstick pointed to her almost non-existent lips, and she wore an electric-blue coat trimmed with fox.

"Oh, Mrs. MacNab, I was sorry to hear about Findlay. How is he?"

"Going to be all right, they say. It's a relief, and that's the truth. As it is I've had to hire a fellow to clean the walks and do the garbage, and with me going up there to the Vic all the time this house is getting simply filthy; would you believe that Mrs. Leblanc up there let one of her kids spill a whole bottle of Coke on the stairs, the pigs people are, it beats me. I've had to take steel wool . . .

So that was back to normal.

Still no knock from Central Europe, thank God. Well, if only he'd keep away and leave me in peace. I was settled in now, it would be an intolerable drag to move. Besides, of course, the expense.

Money became a rather acute problem again that week-end, because I had to spend ten dollars getting a throbbing tooth pulled out, and that left me completely broke, with a week to go till next pension day.

This didn't bother me, specially. I felt, in fact, remarkably cheerful (toothache gone; no more Hungarian rhapsodies), and on the Monday set about seriously looking for things. It was an occupation, and it had its concrete rewards, too. Practice had by now made me a really inventive and ingenious looker, so it was skill, not luck, that took me into the bus-terminus Ladies' toward evening. And there I found not only a crumpled dollar bill, but behind a sink the prettiest ring, set with a blue stone that I knew was a real sapphire. My heart felt lighter than a girl's as I trotted along with it to Sam's. If he offered me anything less than five dollars for it, I'd wear it myself and stay hungry. Always liked a ring with that kind of setting. But he actually gave me nineteen dollars, after a long haggle we both enjoyed.

And I thought to myself, "Now there's enough to eat on hand till my cheque comes, I might just treat myself to a new dress. After all, it's nearly spring. And I'm not dead yet." No, by God, not yet.

Yellow afternoon, a bright glitter on melting snow. A light flutter in the clear air. Crystals of frost stiffening the puddles where gold shone back at the gold sky. And somebody coughing. The rustle of spring in Montreal is always drowned out by the rattle of congested lungs. The MacNab house was full of coughers; I never came in or out at any hour without hearing somebody in a paroxysm. The Leblanc children were the colour of toadstools and more runny-nosed than ever. Old Mr. Cooper bent low over his wife's arm; his frail old hand trembled on the stick.

But as for me, I never felt better. When shopping for the dress, I discovered that somewhere along the way I'd lost about twenty-five pounds. The Blin & Blin hung on me like a tent. In a quite well-cut dress of slate-blue wool off a half-price rack I looked almost slim. Inspired me to wash and trim my straggling hair and mend a pair of stockings. Felt quite brisk and young as I stepped along over the crackle of ice on the path.

Sure enough, somebody was coughing inside the hall, dark after the daffodil sunset outside. A figure bent over the newel post of the stairs, long overcoat trailing. Long, desperate, hacking coughs.

"Now I'll tell you what to do for that, Mr. Horvath," I said. "Mix up a cup of honey, hot water, and whiskey, and drink it blazing hot."

His dark eyes gazed at me mournfully over the banister. His faced looked bleary and swollen, and his nose was bright red.

"Oh, I not bother, thank you," he said hoarsely.

"Come on," I said heartily. "You can manage that —a good cook like you." At once, reproachfully, he broke out coughing worse than ever, and I felt a trifle ashamed, remembering it was more than likely my flood that had given him his cold.

"Well, you come downstairs with me, then, and I'll fix you up with something."

I unlocked the door and he followed me downstairs, still coughing raucously. Set down my shopping bag, fat with a plastic rain-bonnet, a man's handstitched leather glove, and a child's cotton umbrella with "Fiona" written all over it—the day's finds. The kitchen window a square of gold.. Coughing from the armchair where Horvath had folded up like an unstrung puppet. I had no honey, and of course no whiskey, but a big shot of cheap sherry and lots of sugar in boiling water would do as well.

I took it out to him. "Now you try this." He held it for a few minutes looking morosely down into the steam. Odd that I should at first have thought him so old, and later got the impression he was so young. In fact he was somewhere in between, early fifties, probably. The little bald spot showed through a tangle of curls. Something seedy and depleted about him reminded me of the sick old tom I'd taken in the night of the storm. Both of them shared a certain glum mood of withdrawal. He looked into the mug gloomily and sniffed it once, but seemed unwilling to taste it.

"Drink it while it's hot," I said. And left him to it while I went back to the kitchen to heat myself a bowl of soup. There were one or two more eruptions of coughing, then silence. Then a long, rattling snore that shot me into the sitting-room like a bullet. He had fallen asleep, sunk in the armchair with his coat awkwardly hiked up around him. His head was tilted sideways and his mouth was open to show a number of far from attractive teeth. In sleep all his flash and swagger were gone; he was like a clown with the make-up wiped off.

"Damn it," I told myself crossly. "When will you learn? Shove him out."

But somehow I couldn't wake the poor devil up. There was a deep line scored across his wide forehead I'd never noticed when he was awake; he seemed to be thinking deeply in his sleep, pondering sad, human things in his dreams. It was two hours before I could bring myself to rouse him, interrupting a long, resonant, whistling, bleating sequence of snores. Under my nudging hand a blank instant of terror froze him; then he got up at once, obediently, muttered hoarse thanks, and went lurching off up the stairs on feet still clumsy with sleep. But as I locked up after him, I noted with satisfaction that he made it up to his room without coughing once.

And the best of it was that, for a reward, he left me alone. No calls; no knocking in the next days. Sheer gratitude for this made me feel almost affectionate toward him, and whenever I happened to encounter him (soon recovered and jaunty again), I always said "Good day" and "How are you?" with the greatest friendliness. That, as it turned out, was quite a serious mistake.

All dressed for a night walk, unlocked the basement

door to step out, and found the way blocked by two huge market bags on a pair of snowy legs.

"Ah, you home, come back in," he said genially. His bulk backed me firmly down the steps. "You see, I bring you a little something nice for all your kind medicine to the cough. Too late for good-looking ladies to be out alone now anyhow. I make you a gourmet dinner, how about that for a surprise? You come in, sit down, I do all the work. A little drink first to warm the stomach, then I become the chef. You like a little *coquilles St. Jacques* to begin? Then what you say to a good *boeuf Bourguignonne*—and I find some lovely fresh peas from Mexico—French bread still warm—a nice ripe Camembert, a little fruit and coffee. And I buy also a couple of good wines because today is pay-day, you a nice lady, and I want to give you a nice treat."

"Oh, but look, I'm just on my way out—it's nice of you, but perhaps some other time—I really have to go—"

Might as well have saved my breath. He paid no attention whatsoever to my nattering but marched straight to the kitchen and began to unpack his enormous bags of food. He flung off his coat, talking all the time, uncorked a bottle of Tio Pepe and poured us each a glass. Then, tying a dish-towel around his middle, he directed me firmly to a chair, and began opening and shutting cupboard doors briskly and marshalling my scanty army of pots. What with chopping, beating, stirring, clattering dishes, whistling, he made a noise like seven men. In no time pungent smells of scallops baking in cheese, meat browning in garlic butter, and other things, began to fill the apartment, and I felt quite dazed, what with these heady fumes and the powerful sherry.

Meekly I sat in a corner on the unreliable kitchen stool while he cooked away, talking in his broken lingo the whole time.

"You not eating well, I can see that, you know," he

112

told me sternly. "You pretty, but much too thin. You need to eat proper meals for a while. Tins of soup all I see here in the cupboard, that's no good at all. Well, I know you were very sick this winter, but that all over now, you must get fat now. This good meal be a start. Fill up our glasses again, Mrs. What's your own name, anyway? This better than spirits before the good wine, gets the palate ready to taste—" I filled up the glasses generously. The sherry was good, and since it was clear I was now hopelessly trapped, I settled down to make the best of it and drank up.

When I listened again, he was talking about Liszt. "The greatest music ever invented," he said.

"Oh, I don't think so, really. All those heroic posturings—"

"Yes, that just it, heroic. Grandeur. He is not afraid of that. Only petty bourgeois afraid of grandeur, it embarrass them. In Canada, for instance, the great thing is to be decent, quiet, not notice for anything. That is why she will always be tenth-rate nation."

"Oh, come on now, that's rubbish."

"Not! You take a man like De Gaulle, a great man, the greatest man of our time, a man who understand greatness—he come here to visit Canada, and everybody is *embarrass!*"

"Certainly. Because he's an arrogant old ass, meddling in our politics," I said energetically. The sherry had warmed me, or I would never have bothered to argue with the idiot. He only became more loquacious and outrageous than ever, and I found myself pinned down by a long harangue on the necessity of Quebec's independence. At one point, tingling with annoyance, I tried to get down off the stool and leave the kitchen in dignity, but he actually menaced me with a long spoon. I sat down again and poured out more sherry, muttering "Ridiculous. Absurd man. What rubbish you talk. Nonsense." To all of which he paid no attention at all in the grand avalanche of his own argument. At

113

last I began to laugh helplessly, and that brought him up short.

"You laugh at me!" he said, flushing.

"Of course I do. You're so ridiculous, Johnny."

At once his face broke into a radiant smile. "Ah, you look different woman laughing, pretty as a rose. Now you hungry? The *coquilles* are ready. You see now what a perfect chef Johnny can be. We set the table in the other room—I take plates in, you find silver, then I open the wine for it to breathe a little before we taste."

Beaming and enormously pleased with himself, he set the table and served the first course, which I freely admitted to him was superb. The wine had a flower-like fragrance, even in my battered pair of tumblers. The stew was tender and delicious. I ate more than I could, ate till my stomach felt tight, partly to please him and partly because, once started, I couldn't resist the food.

"I am great chef, right?" he demanded.

"You are great chef."

"You eat good meals like this often now. You like a bird with your bright eyes full of laughing, and delicate like a bird, too, a man want to take care of you. I never see your colour so pink and pretty as now. You have lovely skin, fat woman's skin; but you much too thin. A woman should always have four inches of good fat on her everywhere, all over, the Greeks that made Venus knew that. Have more wine. Instead of 'Home Sweet Home' we put up on the wall here *Nos numerus sumus et fruges consumere nati.*"

"What does that mean?"

"It say we human beings are just ciphers, all we good for is to eat fruits of the earth."

"Oh."

"You surprised I know Horace? I go to the university at Pest for five years. I was going to be a professor, but my father died, then I get married and babies come—then it too late. Now I sew schoolbags

114

for little kids, in a country where people think a diploma like a piece of money. It's a crazy life. And Horace knew everything about it."

At this point, to my dismay, he reached across the table and took my hand in a firm grip. I tried to pry it away, but he held on so powerfully I couldn't extricate myself without an undignified struggle. So I tried to pass it off lightly. He couldn't have any serious intentions—not with an old woman like me.

"Well, that was a very good meal and I feel pounds fatter already. Now how about some coffee—shall I make it?"

"No, no, I do it, women always make terrible coffee. You wait here. I have also little surprise to go with it."

The surprise was a bottle of rosy liqueur I'd never tasted before called Doulce France—a bouquet of raspberries in a fiery syrup that was not too sweet.

"Beautiful, for a beautiful lady," he said, pouring me another.

"I shouldn't, but it is lovely."

"Then you should. Why you not kinder to yourself? Don't you know how special woman you are—wise and funny and warm. And sometimes sad like a little girl nobody invite to a party. Nobody before ever tell you these things?"

I retreated warily to a straight chair with my glass, but he settled cosily on the floor at my feet, head leaning against my knees. There was a silence. The church bells in the next street sounded, and the cool notes rang like music on the quiet air. I touched his curly hair lightly. Oh, I had been imprudent with the wine, on top of too much sherry, and now the sweet fire of Doulce France undermined me; no doubt that was why, when he firmly tugged me down to the floor beside him, I had no organized defence ready at all. Confused and dismayed, I found myself at once engulfed in some very direct preliminaries.

"Yes, you have beautiful skin, like silk," he murmured, his mouth on my neck. I was pinned under him. Consternation kept me still once I realized I hadn't the strength to get free.

"No—look—really—don't—" I said foolishly.

My stupid head was spinning. His mouth covering mine was warm, gentle and warm, sweet and warm. On the floor his body covered mine, warm and patient, warm and loving. His eyes looked down into mine, in amusement and tenderness. He seemed to see me there, me myself, and greet me with delight, and I had the absurd illusion that no man had ever before looked at and really seen me, in friendship as well as desire. My head was turning, my blood had begun to run warm. He was drowning me then in a sweet, familiar pleasure I thought I'd forgotten all about, that hadn't existed for me since Burt turned it all into ugliness and hate those many years ago.

After it was over I lay beside him drowsily, drifting near sleep in a peaceful place where old attitudes and convictions had little or no reality. I felt remotely pleased, serene and amused. Just fine, in fact.

"Yes, I was right about you," he said comfortably. "You like a girl, shy, a bit lonesome, but full of mysteries, full of loving."

"I'm nearly old enough to be your mother, you know."

"You young enough for me."

"You have a few surprises yourself. Ridiculous man."

"Ridiculous you. Yes, you beautiful for loving, I knew that first time I see you. Asked you to marry me. You think I forget that. Of course I was drunk. But I try many times to come and be your friend. And I was right. You like me, don't you? You like my body, too? Yes, I know you do."

"I suppose I'd better get up off here . . ."

"No, no, stay with me. This almost the nicest part of it, to lie together and talk."

"Mm. Well . . ."

"You comfortable?"

"Yes. Too comfortable. Also slightly drunk, I'm

116

afraid." And privately rather glad of it, because I knew tomorrow's regrets were only waiting to pounce and punish a shameless old woman, lying on the floor half dressed after intercourse with a stranger. But I only had time to think with a private giggle, What, oh what, would Mrs. MacNab say?, before I fell into a warm, deep sleep.

Q. You actually let him—?

A. I even helped.

Q. How could you?

A. Twice. Or maybe it was three times.

Q. You were drunk at the time, of course.

A. Oh yes. But not too drunk, if you see . . . anyway, that's no excuse. It isn't a reason, either. Something about him . . .

Q. Polish, isn't he?

A. No, Hungarian.

Q. Never mind. Speaks fractured English.

A. Yes. And too much of it.

Q. Young enough to be your son, too.

A. Yes.

Q. Works in a factory?

A. Yes.

Q. That makes it worse, somehow, doesn't it?

A. Oh yes, I'm afraid so. Class systems never die.

Q. So you have committed—

A. Fornication, that's right. Adultery, too, come to that. Unfaithful to Burt for the first time. Or do I mean last? Anyhow, guilty.

Q. On the floor.

A. Yes. Twice or three times. Didn't even take off our shoes.

Q. Tcha. And would you tell the court, please, just what the hell you plan to do now?

A. I don't know. Go away from here, I suppose. But at my age it does seem a bit crazy to run away twice in the same year from two different men.

117

Q. Does it occur to you the place to run is back home?

A. No. Frankly, it doesn't.

Q. But what now? You can't possibly allow this kind of thing to go on, can you?

A. I suppose not.

Q. Even if we forget all the rest of it (which we can't), he's an impossible fellow, isn't he?— egoistic, argumentative, ridiculous, irritating—

A. Yes, all that. Much more, too. Primitive and also highly intelligent. Intriguing combination. He's been battered, but he hasn't lost his compassion. Not rough and crude; just natural. Surprising how rare that is. When I woke up he was gone, but there was a pillow under my head and a blanket over me. And he'd done the dishes.

Q. Remind me how old you are.

A. All right, all right. Sixty-six next fall.

Q. Indecent, so much sentiment at your time of life. And you haven't answered my other question—what now?

A. Don't know.

Q. This mustn't happen again, right? Sordid. Unseemly. Admit you feel ashamed when you think of it.

A. I do. But—

Q. Then it musn't happen again.

A. No, I suppose not. You're right. It was sordid.

Q. And besides, the point is, you wanted to be free. Didn't you?

A. Yes, that's the point. I did.

Q. And you still do?

A. Yes.

Q. Then when do you plan to get out of here?

A. Well, whenever this hang-over lets up. Say next week.

Q. That's settled, then. After all, if you haven't got self-respect, what have you got?

A. Right. I guess.
Q. Now look here. You admit it's obscene, an old woman like you—
A. Yes, yes. Even if he does say I'm beautiful for loving.
Q. Was he sober at the time?
A. No, of course not.
Q. Well, then?
A. Oh, do shut up.
Q. Hundreds of rooms for rent in the paper.
A. Yes, I know it.
Q. Impossible, anything else. You know that, too.
A. Yes, yes. Absolutely. I plead guilty, I tell you. Temporary insanity. Promise to reform. I'll start looking for a room at once. Well, tomorrow. Now will you *kindly* piss off and leave me alone.

It was the last thing I expected him to do next: namely, nothing. Most disconcerting. A big vacuum of silence that took me right off guard. Days of it went by. Never saw a whisker of him. No knocking. Nothing whatsoever left of that night except a smile that tickled my lips from time to time, and a touch of stiffness in the hams. Sorted through my things in a languid kind of way, and discarded some. Dragged out the suitcase, looked at it, and kicked it under the bed again. Read the ads for rooms and made big, firm rings around a few with pencil, then felt too tired to go out. Sleet fell, a nasty, rapping noise like coffin nails.

Of course it was obvious. He'd done a few questions and answers himself. What would he want, a fellow full of ideas and sap like that, with a queer old female scavenger living out of tins, somebody foreign to him in every way, and on top of all that, a snob? He'd been a bit drunk, that's all. Forgotten all about it by now, without a doubt. And very sensible of him, too. Much the best thing to do. It made no sense for me to move out—what need was there? We could come and go our separate ways as we'd done for months before, and with a bit of luck never lay eyes on each other. If we did, a polite nod, a word about the weather. What could be simpler?

There was some comfort in this, but not as much as there should have been. It was a real effort to pick up and go shopping or looking for things as usual. I found nothing, either, for days and days—seemed to have lost the knack. Legs ached on the slippery streets. The east wind was raw. Ice in the roads black. But staying home was just as bad, pushing away the silence with books or music on the radio, trying not to listen for a knock on the door.

Well, that's that, I thought. Forget it, please. You were happy as a bedbug before. Now be happy again, damn you. So, with some effort, I got through the days, and gradually felt better. It took quite a little while, and the bitter March wind and rain were no help, but I really did settle down eventually and began to get some fun out of my excursions again. Felt quite smug and proud of myself.

And then, of course, one night there was a knock at the door, and at once my heart flopped over on its side like some fatuous old spaniel.

Might as well answer it, I thought, after a second of doubt. Have to encounter him some time, and make one or two things quite clear. Sooner the better, really. So I opened the door and let him in. He was carrying a coffee-pot steaming at the spout, but he brought it in with none of his usual panache. In fact, he looked so depressed I hardly recognized him. Even his curls hung low with dejection. He was unshaven, and the heavy bristles gave him a gloomy, disreputable air.

"Well, what's wrong with *you?*"

"With me, you ask. Everything. Everything."

He clapped the pot carelessly down on a side-table and threw himself into the one armchair.

"Well, what does that mean?"

120

"I lose my job last week, that's all. Also other problems I never tell you about. But I have a big bust-up with the boss, and now no job."

"Oh."

"He is Lithuanian," he added, as if that explained everything.

"But why did he fire you?"

Galvanized, he shot to his feet and began a long tirade I found all but impenetrable. It seemed to boil down to the fact he had been asked to work overtime and had refused.

"Well, that's too bad, but with your experience I suppose you can always get another job. In fact, I wonder why you don't try to get into teaching or do translation work; you have the education for it and surely it would be more—"

"No, no, a teacher is a slave, marking bits of paper all night, and these white-collar jobs you like so much, what are they but prisons, somebody tell you what to do, when to wake up mornings, how long to wear your hair. In my work you free, can think or sing at the machine, then go away free. I know what you think, though. That kind of work has no prestige. You like better a man of profession, not just a stitcher on leather. What I am matters nothing, only what position I have. Is that what you feel? No, for sure not, Eva, you too wise for that, aren't you? You not just kind . . ."

When I made no comment, he remarked, "You very cool."

"Am I?"

"So I suppose you think Johnny a bum, might as well treat him cool like everybody else. What has he got, after all? Nothing. Nothing at all. Forty-eight years and two empty hands. No wife, no children, no country. And now not even his crummy job. Just a bum. Of course you despise me."

"No," I said, unwillingly touched in spite of myself by these histrionics. "Here, have some coffee."

But he sat still with head between his hands, bitterly staring down at the floor.

"Nothing to look forward to," he muttered. "No future. No hope to have a home, see my family again. Sometimes I wish I never leave Hungary, even with the Soviets there. In Hungary I was somebody. I had so much. My mother still there, she is old and may be dead, between one letter and the next I never know, can hardly remember the sound of their voices or how in our flat the rooms go. Here I am alone. I am nothing and I have nothing."

"Drink up your coffee, Johnny."

He gave me a brooding flash from the dark eyes. "Yes, you want me to go. I am a nuisance. You cold, unfriendly, *English* tonight."

"Look; I'm not, it's only that—"

"You turn me out too, because now I have no job."

"No, no, you don't—"

"And yet I make you that beautiful dinner."

Half laughing, I touched him helplessly on the hunched shoulder. "It was a beautiful dinner. I'm sorry about your job, but it's surely not the end of the world, is it? Why couldn't you go to the boss and simply ask him to take you back?"

"Never."

"But I'm sure he doesn't want to lose a good man like you. You're a skilled workman, after all."

"I am first-rate," he said fiercely, "but I sooner die than go back there apologize to that Lithuanian bastard."

"Oh, he wants an apology."

"I tell you, he wait till the end of the world for it."

"Oh, Johnny, what do you care? Don't you know it takes a big man to apologize?"

"Never," he repeated. But he rubbed his hands through his hair, sat up, and gulped down some of his coffee. A few minutes later, when I came along to refill his cup, he took hold of me and tried to pull me down into his lap.

122

"No, Johnny," I said with great firmness. "Now I want you to get something straight. You know what happened that night was just—well just—I mean, it can't happen again. We both had a bit too much to drink . . . you understand, I like you very much, but just as a neighbour and a friend. Let's keep it that way, all right?"

Except for being ridiculous, it wasn't a bad little speech. The trouble was, he didn't appear to hear a word of it, but ran his two hands firmly up my legs as I stood there with the coffee-cups. A subversive pleasure crept through my veins. I stiffened in protest and pulled away; but at the same moment saw that tears were making a bright track down the bristled cheek that had been pressed against my knee.

After that, it didn't seem to matter. We lay together on the sofa, and this time it was slow and friendly, natural as breathing, without embarrassment or thinking or any words at all. We both slept afterwards comfortably together under the blankets. Vaguely in the grainy light of dawn I saw him dress and go. Then I fell asleep again.

When I woke, it was a state of perfect simplicity. There were no questions, and no answers. No plans. No regrets. Only a sense of happiness flickering like sunlight in my old hands and cheeks and belly and all over.

"Who's that woman with the two pasty children that lives upstairs?"

"You mean Jeanne Leblanc."

"I met her coming in just now; one of the kids tried to give me a disgusting bit of candy and she dragged him away with such a dirty look you'd think I had leprosy. What's wrong with her, anyhow—her face is yellow as butter."

"Poor thing, she's pregnant again. Her husband, he

123

got the priest after her so she stopped taking the pill, you know that one."

"They must be idiots, both of them. One of those kids looks retarded as it is. But the way she glared at me, you'd think it was all my fault."

"She jealous, maybe. Because you can make love and not get a full belly."

"I'm getting fat again just the same. It's awful. These meals of yours are swelling me up like a toad."

"I tell you fat is good. I like your round belly. What you want, to be like those poor skin-and-elbow Mac-Nabs? Did you know those two don't eat enough to feed a rat? Always buy day-old bread to save, use tea-bags twice, meat just once a week—and all to feed this house, pay the mortgage and taxes and like that. What a reason to keep thin. Of course, it's all they have, but the house owns them; they spend their whole life for it like slaves."

"Where's Mr. MacNab, if any?"

"In the Kingston Penitentiary."

"Oh."

"He walk out on her when Findlay was three. But after that he used to come back sometimes and take away all her money. You know those days a woman had no property in Quebec, could have no separate bank account, even, so she couldn't stop him. She was happy as a queen the day we read in the paper he sentenced to fourteen years. I never once saw her smile till that day, poor bitch."

"Hmph."

"As for poor old Findlay, he never smile at all. He is only his mother's shadow, poor bugger. Thirty years old and he thinks it's only to pee out of, never had a girl or a holiday or did one crazy thing in all his life. But you know what he did last winter? I talk to him about it, and he start a night course in oil painting, how you think of that?"

"Surprised."

"I go there myself, four or five years now, paint big

124

canvases, just for fun, play with the shapes and colours."

"You never told me that. Or showed me any of your pictures."

"They very bad."

"Funny to hear you being shy. But what a lot you know about everybody here."

"Well, I live here eight years after all. I like poor old Findlay. Tomorrow I take him up a little sip of rye to the hospital. It do him good to break some rules. And the Leblancs are next door to me. When they go out I listen, make sure the kids are okay. And I sometimes play chess with that taxi-driver André, the one with the poodle, who live with his friend up on the top floor. The poodle is a girl called Fleurette, I like that."

"Me too."

"And that nice old Mrs. Cooper in the front rooms, you know for Christmas she give me a scarf she knits herself. What a life she has with that crabby old man, except that she love the old bugger. She taught music for thirty years at the Collège Marie de France, you should hear her play Liszt, even with those old hands. They have a daughter married to a rich American, she never comes near them or sends a little present, only a cheque each month. Some child, eh? But you never hear Mrs. Cooper say one word to complain, never."

"Johnny, you're a gossip."

"A gossip! Is that a bad thing, to know about people? I like knowing all about them. What you rather talk about? The roast chicken I have in the oven? Yes, you like food, don't you? You want giblet gravy with, or bread sauce? Or you rather talk about bed and what a first-rate lover Johnny is? Ah, I love to see you blush. . . . "

"You're the one should be blushing, you layabout. Sitting around here every night with your shoes off, gabbing. When are you going to see that Mr. Litvak about getting your job back?"

"Yes, yes, I go Monday. Let's have a drink."

"There's hardly any left. You had most of it yesterday. You drink too much."

"Nag, nag. What a woman you are."

"Well, I drink too much myself these days, for that matter. You're a bad influence. All right; let's finish the bottle off."

"Why not? I still have ten dollars in the bank."

"Rich and reckless John Horvath."

"That's right, laugh. Let me hear you laugh."

Monday was a broad, beaming day full of light and the flash of water running blue under the sun. At the edge of every grimy crust of snow around the house shone a margin of wet green grass. The air was so clear that, looking east, you could see the red peak of the Jacques Cartier bridge and think about the green water under it, clotted with melting ice, flowing fast out of the Gulf, out to the blue sea.

Treated myself to an egg roll and tea for lunch at a little Chinese place near Sam's. Glad to get inside; the wind was bitter for all the blaze of sun, and a straggling queue of schoolgirls being herded to a Lenten mass gaped and giggled as red-nosed me stumped past them in torn coat and dirty tennis shoes. Orientals are politer, or their faces are better designed to conceal amusement; I was bowed to a booth table like a queen.

Someone had kindly left a *Gazette* on the bench, but I didn't bother to open it. Nothing of much importance there. I wondered how Johnny was managing his interview with Mr. Litvak. Very badly, no doubt. But he was a few degrees less bull-headed about the whole thing now than he'd been ten days ago, and a lot less demoralized. It all might help. Certainly he'd set out in a mood of fine, careless confidence. "He apologize to me, I apologize to him," he told me comfortably, and clearly he thought this the epitome of sweet reasonableness. Which perhaps it was.

Had planned a quite long and ambitious excursion for the afternoon, down to the railway station where the finding was generally good, specially when the flood of commuters subsided after rush hour. At first I'd been timid about going down there, it's such a public sort of cross-road for the whole city, but one day I found a pair of big owl-round dark glasses and knew that behind them I was safe—no one on earth or off it would ever recognize me. Of course, with my head bundled in a canary-yellow muffler (found in a Woolworth's loo), the effect of these glasses was a little arresting, but I'd pretty well given up caring about things like that.

Today, though, it was a bit hard to concentrate. You have to focus your attention and imagination to find things. And mine kept wandering off to Johnny and his job and speculations about both. The afternoon was just about middle-aged when my back began to ache and I decided to head back home. Hadn't found a single thing, either, all that bus fare wasted. But he might just get back early. Or perhaps stay late in a fever of goodwill, to do overtime. Whichever it was, I was curious to hear about it. There was a bit of hamburger left in the frig, and one or two onions; he'd make something savoury out of it for supper. That's if he didn't arrive in glum defeat. . . .

The evening shadows stretched out slim and lazy. The sun dropped like a red coin down a slit of cloud. Street lamps opened round eyes in the blue dusk. No sign of Johnny yet. I was hungry, but didn't want to eat before he came in. Shifted myself restlessly from window to window, none of them the slightest help. Full dark and still no sign of him. Then later, moon bright, the house quiet. My back hurt. Crossly I opened a tin of soup and ate some of it. No doubt the lunatic had gone off somewhere drinking to celebrate with his cronies. He seemed to know thousands of people, most of them, as far as I could gather, deplorable. It would be just like him to get colossally drunk his first day back on the job. There was something primitive, even wild, about the man. Refugee neurosis, I would have said in my N.D.G. days, when I had convenient labels for everything. He seemed so simple at first, almost a clown; now I knew him better, it seemed to me I'd never met a man before quite so complicated, such a collection of paradoxes—absurd and wise, funny and profound, animal and thinker. Even his moods were mixed, and shifted from minute to minute like light changing. There was something vivid and vital about the creature, even when he was fast asleep. Well, in whatever mood or condition, he'd better not come crashing drunk down my stairs again. I checked to make sure the door upstairs was locked, after first unlocking it quietly and having a brief listen. Only the normal house noises. Mrs. Cooper tinkling "To a Wild Rose" on the piano, a Leblanc child crying, a crackle of TV gunfire, Findlay's new, slow bedroom slippers in the back hall. I closed and locked the door briskly and went downstairs to bed. Time to sleep. Put out the light. Put up a short prayer. Reverend Sir: Finding very poor today. Please improve same. Make crazy Johnny all right. And make me a good girl, if at all possible. And oblige. Amen.

Back gnawing like a rat's tooth. Damn the thing. Wind rising . . . not more snow—P.S., God: Please no more snow.

Never fear, Johnny would be around again soon enough. Actually a treat to have the place to myself for a change, after having him underfoot so much of the time lately with his incessant and generally maddening conversation. What was that he said the other day about fluorine in water making people bald—or was it sterile? They didn't have fluorine in the water in Hungary when he was young, you see. He also is convinced that there's life on Mars, and a potato in

128

your pocket cures rheumatism. The most ridiculous man in the whole solar system.

The long wail of a siren, the voice of disaster. Back no easier. House as full of high-pitched silence as an empty box. Hungry; used to more than a tin of soup for dinner. I often slept poorly; this was nothing new. Nuisance not finding anything today. Funds getting low; he's turning me into an epicure with all this expensive eating and drinking. Better luck tomorrow, I hope. Back will be better . . . unless that's more damn snow coming down out there. Fine night to be out carousing, I must say. Think he'd know better at his age. As long as he doesn't get fired again. . . . A good thing if he keeps long working-hours for a while, let me get on with my own doings. What a head he'll have tomorrow, the fool. Well, good luck to him, wherever he lies. No doubt I'll hear the whole improbable story soon enough. And at very great length. Now go to sleep.

Cheerful and free as the wind all next day. There had been no new snow after all, and my back felt better. Found a boy's bruised algebra book with a couplet scribbled in the flyleaf: "I know two things about the horse,/And one of them is rather coarse." Also, sticking out of some dirty, melting snow, a heavy silver tablespoon smuggled from home by some small child for use as a shovel. Sam gave me eighty-five cents for it, and I bought a head of crisp, green lettuce and a little bunch of bright daffodils because their frilled horns and star of bland petals gave me so much pleasure. The fat Chinese woman in the dirty green-grocer's apron had a face expressionless as a bum, but as she wrapped and handed me the flowers I saw at once that she was brimming with a secret, wild urge to laugh. That tickled me, I don't know why. It didn't matter what the joke was—or that it was perhaps on me; it was enough that there was a joke.

129

Home at dusk, pleasantly tired. Put the daffodils in a glass. Made a face at black tom through the kitchen window, at which the old ram rose politely to his stiff legs and made a bow. Went to some trouble then to whack open the bathroom window and push out a bit of left-over sausage to him. Turned on the radio and left it on, in spite of the gushes of Franz Liszt perversely chosen by the program director. Washed out the yellow muffler, which needed it, and, because laundry is so contagious, hung up stockings and a sweater to drip too.

Several times thought I heard a knock at the door and went out to the foot of the stairs to listen; but no one was there. Well, with the hang-over he so richly deserved, he was no doubt having an early night for a change. I went to bed early myself with a copy of *Cranford*, and soon fell asleep.

Just at the first lifting of the dark, I woke up sharply, flesh rough and heart drumming. Not a sound anywhere. No memory of a dream. Everything quiet and normal outside. But inside, a queer and mounting sense of crisis too vague to name, too strong to shake off. Couldn't get back to sleep. Couldn't read: the chapter called "Panic" no longer seemed funny. As soon as the light came, I got dressed, but couldn't settle to anything. After a while, fidgeted out; came in again; and went out, always dogged by a sort of restless alertness without focus. Sometimes it receded to a dim sort of malaise; other times it was discomfort sharp as a hangnail. Made no difference how I reasoned with and scolded it; the feeling refused to go away.

Only once in my life before had I felt anything like it, and that was the spring when May wrote me—her scrawl even more obscure than usual—that she'd recently had a nasty fall on some stairs. She mentioned dizzy spells and a bit of trouble with her eyes. Nothing, she said cheerfully, but what we ladies so portentously call The Change. Lorne, she added, had unkindly suggested she was drinking too much, and she'd consequently told him to go to Albany, and stay there. "Don't worry," she added up the side of the page. "I'm not and he won't." There was really nothing in this to alarm anyone specially, but I couldn't lose a nagging, irrational anxiety about her. For weeks I heard nothing more. On several nights I tried to reach her with a long-distance call, but no one answered the phone in her apartment. Finally, after a tart exchange of differing views with Burt, I actually went up to New York on the bus one night to see her for myself.

It was still early in June, but the city was shimmering in a humid jungle heat. At five in the morning the temperature was already ninety. The air felt like rubber, and the tarry roads, soft with heat, smelled acid. When I could get no answer at May's apartment door, I pushed the janitor's button, and a tall Negress came panting up from below with perspiration glittering on her dark face.

"Oh, that lady been in hospital quite a while," she said. "They come one night and take her in an ambulance—quite sick, I guess she is. Which one? Well, I just happen to hear her friend say somethin' about Doctors' Hospital, that's a private place, I don't know just where it is. . . . "

I wasn't surprised to hear bad news; it even gave me a grim sort of satisfaction to know that interminable bus ride had been justified. But nothing prepared me, after a long ride uptown on a torrid, leather taxi-seat, for the sight of May herself. The floor nurse gave me a professional look and said, "Yes, she had an operation ten days ago to remove a tumour."

"What—was it a brain tumour?"

"Yes."

"Was it malignant?"

"Her condition is satisfactory," the nurse said blandly. "You can talk to her; it's good for her to be roused. You'll find her rather drowsy. Now, Miss

131

Clark, here's a visitor for you. Do you know who this lady is? Can you tell me her name?"

"But this is the wrong room," I thought at first. Because the figure on the bed was not only not May, it was not really anybody. There was no identity in the long body, naked under the hospital sheet; there was no gender and no age in the skull covered with dark bristles, the long, thin arms crossed, hands making small, delicate, meaningless movements. The drowsy, blank eyes looked into mine without curiosity.

"It's Blossom Hendry," she said. Then her upper lip lifted in a yawn and her eyes closed. The nurse rustled away. I sat down by the bed and took May's hand—a fan of light twig-bones, dry and warm and indifferent.

"Honey, how do you feel?"

She opened her eyes then. Recognition flickered there for a moment. After a pause she said in a dragging voice, "Bloody, thanks, Eva."

"They say you're doing very well," I told her, but the sound of my false, bright words appalled me, and I said no more. Her eyes closed again. After a few minutes I got up and stood by the high bed helplessly. What can possibly be said that has any interest or meaning to the dying? Nothing, surely. Nothing at all.

"Good-bye, love," I said, touched the indifferent cheek with a kiss, and went away.

Luckily that had been my only experience till now of premonition. There can't be a more dispensable gift in this booby-trap-ridden life. But all next day (still no Johnny seen or heard from), I couldn't lose that stubborn feeling of something wrong, persistent as an itch. It gave me no peace, though I did all sorts of energetic things to shake it off, like scrub the tennis shoes. (They looked worse than ever.) As night came on, I felt lower and lower; it was like sinking into a frosty black hole of time. Finally, very late, I wrestled my feet into the damp shoes, and went shivering down the dark street to find a phone booth. If it was Neil or

Kim, or even Burt—I wanted to know. Had to know. Much bother getting change, dialling the wrong number several times with stiff, trembly fingers. Then the phone rang and rang at the other end. The Fates seemed to be out or dead. Nobody else seemed to care.

At last a click. My son's sleep-furred voice.

"Neil? It's Mother. Sorry about the hour—I just thought I'd call to see if you were all right. Are you?"

"For God's sake, Mum. It's one-thirty in the morning! Yes, of course I'm all right. Where are you?"

"In a phone booth. Don't be cross, dear. I just suddenly felt like saying hello. Kim told me you were worried that time we ran into each other . . . and I just thought I'd give you a call. To see if you were all right."

"Yes, I'm fine. That is, I'm as fine as can be expected." He breathed into the receiver. "Kim told me all about that. It bothered her a lot that you looked so . . . neglected. And of course it bothered the hell out of me to hear it. Mother, when are you coming home?"

"Oh, I didn't call you to talk about all that, Neil. Just to hear your voice."

"But you can't go on living like this, Mum—"

"Please. Just tell me how you are, dear. In detail."

He gave a little snort that might have been a laugh. "Why, middle-aged. Short of breath in heavy traffic. I get heartburn at breakfast-time. Cold sweat as income-tax deadline approaches, Occasional impotence. That answer your question?"

Irony was a novel art to him; it made him sound a new man, and considerably more interesting than the old one.

"Where are you? Not in bed."

"No, I fell asleep in the study. Working out my tax forms."

"I see. Kim and the boys all right?"

"They're fine. Kim's average for her age, I guess.

133

Bitchy, beautiful, sulky, in love with a shaggy oaf in dirty leather clothes. Her mother wants to send her to St. Helen's School in the Townships."

"Don't," I said.

"No, I won't. I want my own eye on her. Rosemary's taken a sleeping pill. She isn't very well these days. Nerves."

"Mm. I can imagine."

"Mother, no kidding, are you all right? Why don't you admit you've had enough of this—whatever it is. You're ready to come back now, aren't you? Dad's been so depressed, it's a misery to see him. He even bought a dog."

Bit my cheeks hard to keep in the guffaw that fought to get out.

"You're not crying, are you?" he asked suspiciously.

"No. Not crying. How's his arthritis?"

"Oh, about the same. We finally found a very decent woman to keep house—after a series of goons you wouldn't believe—but this woman's a widow, a Mrs. Pratt from Ontario. Fiftyish, I.O.D.E. and all that. He seems to get on with her well, though she's a little tiny woman and we've had to get in a char for the heavy work twice a week."

"So it's worked out fairly well."

"He wouldn't say so."

"No, but he wouldn't even if it were true."

"Maybe. But what about you? Are you telling the truth, Mum? You want to come home, don't you?"

My turn now to breathe. "No, I don't."

"You know, of course, you can. Any time. Just come."

"Yes, but I won't be doing that. It's all over. You must know that by this time. So must Burt, even if he won't admit it. No, I'm all right as I am; just fine, in fact. I like my life as it is."

"That, Mum, I honestly find hard to believe. So did Kim."

"Mostly it's true," I said after a painful pause. "Of

134

course, sometimes I feel a bit low. You know something about that nowadays yourself, don't you? Whatever you do there's a price . . . and amputations ache. I admit that. Got myself all worked up in a worry about you tonight, for instance, and had to call you at this crazy hour. But it's the best talk, in some ways, we've ever had, and I feel better now. There's not the remotest chance of my going back; you'll just have to accept that, dear."

A silence while he absorbed this. "Can't I do anything to help you?" he asked finally. "Money or anything you need?"

"Not a thing, thanks. Just to talk to you once in a while, specially like this when you're alone and it's all spontaneous, as it were."

"I'd rather see you. Why don't we—"

"No, dear. It's all too complicated to explain. But I'll just ring you from time to time, if that's not a nuisance. I just like to be sure you're all right."

"I'm all right, Mum."

"So am I. Well, good-night now, my dear."

"Good-night. Bless you."

Walking back in the jaws of a bitter night wind, I wiped away tears that made the street lamps jump and splinter; but that nagging sense of dread was eased, and once home I slept for eight unbroken hours.

Thankless swine. Lump of Hungarian mud. Not even the common decency—let alone good manners—six days without so much as a—great, ever-talking bore. To think I put up with it! Loafing around here, swilling drink and pigging down food, arguing about Shakespeare and supermarkets and Siamese cats. Him and his gourmet meals! Somebody should have marinated him years ago, maybe they will yet, food-mill him to a fine mush and season with dill. Well, it serves me right for fraternizing with a nut who believes in faith healing and the superiority of the male. Imagine

135

wasting five minutes with anybody who is *sure* Queen Elizabeth was a man ... I mean a genuine zany, reciting Heine one minute and putting a spell on the cat the next. Just the kind of idiot to disappear permanently for no reason at all, like a case of hives.

People slide curious eyes at me. Am I talking out loud? Well, what if I am. Let them hear. Take a message. Bohunk, wizard, stay away from my door. I mean for ever. You irritate me, even *in absentia*.

After all these years of experience, too; you'd think I could have recognized him on sight for a Class A nit. A separatist. A believer in witchcraft. Admirer of Mussolini. Reader of palms. Cook. Without even the grace, after all I've done for him, even to ...

Well, the best thing he could do for me—and the whole race—would be to vanish like a bad smell. Get off my back, anyhow, like the tick he is. Found half a book of bus tickets in the mud today. I'll travel and forget. Where to, lady? Safari to Montreal West, or the romantic subway to the northlands of Henri Bourassa Street ... anywhere. Emigrate. Find a better hole. Excellent idea. Simply disappear myself. Getting very bored with the MacNab environment. Scenery all right, but natives too restless. Immigrants specially deplorable. No idea how to behave. Vomit on your stairs one minute and disappear the next, without so much as a good-bye fart. ...

And a very good evening to you, madam. What's the matter, never seen a pair of sunglasses before? Silly cow.

Silly man. Nothing more contemptible, after all, than silliness in a man. A flyweight. Erratic as a waterbug. Here today, there tomorrow, no waving goodbye. Not even a gaudy postcard. That is, I suppose he hasn't to anyone. Of course with a nut like that, you never know.

Ah there, pregnant Mrs. L. Sallow as buttermilk yet, I see, and just as sour. What's the matter, haven't you seen him either?

Ugh, a touch of heartburn myself.

Place smells of mould.

The hell with soup. Maybe later. Cold down here, too. The MacNabs saving on oil, no doubt.

Time I got out of here, all right. Me for the bus first thing tomorrow. Serious room-hunt. An attic this time —get some light, at least, after this dark hole. And absolutely No Hungarians. Leave your bull outside.

On your left, Ladies and Gentlemen, in N.D.G., a very neat suburb of hell. Note those rows of bright, ugly, cheap shops—cleaner's, shoe-repair place, Greek restaurant, costume-jeweller, drugstore—comments, every one, on how limited, after all, are the needs of the human spirit. Observe the pot-holes and unre-moved snow: much city graft in Our Lady's domain.

So this was the land of lost delights, I thought, staring curiously out of the dusty bus window. Every inch of every block was familiar—I grew up here, when the trees in N.D.G. Park were just new-planted twigs; never lived anywhere else all my married life. It was a solemn thought. Nearly seventy years in philodendron-land; Reader's Digestville; two-storey-dom. On streets called Draper, Wilson, Harvard, and Grove Hill Place, where, till recently, the French language was never heard, and people were too respect-able to sit out on the front porch in the evenings. And I was quite content there. Even, for some years, more or less happy. Which is, of course, the hell of it.

I got off on Monkland Avenue and adjusted the tinted glasses before setting off to walk west. Men all off at work; only women about, moving in and out of shop-doors with serious, earnest faces. Past the super-market where I knew every tin, and every tin knew me. What I was looking for, what on earth I had in mind, eluded me; but it was simple curiosity that dragged me irresistibly down the street where Burt and I had lived so long—where he and the Daughter

137

of the Empire and the dog still lived. My heart thumped heavily. This was a crazy thing to do. Some- one might recognize me in spite of the shoes and the dark glasses. Was that what I wanted?—to be known and recaptured?

The house looked absolutely different. No, of course not absolutely; but different enough to open my eyes round in surprise. New curtain on the front door— ecru lace, if you please. My plants all gone from the bay window. Dog-prints on the snowy path. Well! I jogged on past, not daring to slow down enough to take in any more. No wish to encounter the house- keeper, dainty Mrs. Pratt, coming in or out with her —my—shopping-basket. Very odd to have a key in my purse and yet go on past. Very odd.

Neil was just over two when we bought the place, for four thousand dollars. Big price in those days. And at that we had to borrow most of the down pay- ment. It took hours and hours of anxious calculation every month, and plenty of scrimping, to meet the mortgage payments and the taxes. Place free and clear now, of course. And it was worth four times as much now; a good investment, and that gave Burt so much satisfaction. But he'd always loved the place for other reasons, too, been proud of it, cherished it like a per- son. He did all the repairs himself, always, before the arthritis, and redecorated personally every three years. That house was his achievement made visible; it was an extension of himself, in fact, and, as such, not to be despised.

I was pregnant when we moved in, and always thought it was the mess and fatigue of moving that brought on the miscarriage, so from the first I didn't feel really friendly to the place. Thought it a bit cramped and never liked the narrow front windows or the steep stairs. Still, in those grim Depression years it was something to be a homeowner and free of the annual May moving, when two-thirds of the city simultaneously tried to fit into a cheaper place to live.

"You ought to be thankful," was always Burt's refrain, whenever I criticized or complained of his dear house. And I believed him. I tried to be thankful, and for years succeeded. We still hoped for more children, in spite of two more disappointments not to be blamed on the house. Neil was eight when I developed a kidney condition in another pregnancy, and the doctor advised an abortion.

"Oh, but I don't think I could do that—"

"Now look, there a high risk; if you come to term with this one you may lose your own life. After all, you have one child, Eva, and he needs you. Talk it over with your husband, of course, but—I'm sending you along to a specialist, but I know what he'll say. The thing to do is come into hospital and I'll tie off your tubes."

Burt, grimly worried that winter and struggling with a series of carbuncles as well as a pay-cut, urged me to take the doctor's advice, and I finally did. But after the operation I was so listless and depressed he was more worried than ever. His solicitude followed me anxiously everywhere. There was no money for a holiday, of course, not in those depressed times; but he gave up smoking, and all summer walked the four miles to his office downtown to save tram fare. That was how he scraped the money to build a sunporch onto the back of the house, where I could raise my plants and keep my books.

Yes, I had the decency to be thankful. And it was a long time before either of us realized how sterile gratitude is. Right to the end, though, it was that neat, middle-class little house that was the chief thing we shared. One of the few things we could discuss amicably was buying things for it, like a coat of paint or new aluminum windows. So I helped to build my own prison.

Trotted along faster and faster, pursued by these reflections, until I found myself back on Monkland Avenue. Breath a bit short. Felt inexplicably upset.

What on earth had brought me back here, scruffy old Enoch Arden that I was. Did I seriously think of living in this district again? Could Neil be right—did I really want to go back home?

Sun high now; felt hot and fussed with hurrying; streets were full of shoving, chattering school kids out for lunch. They made my head spin with their brutal energy, their sureness about everything. It was a huge relief to clamber onto the bus and roll away.

That afternoon I went along to see a bright little two-room apartment over a variety store on Pie Neuf Boulevard, and put a small deposit on it for when it would fall vacant on the first of May. Doing this gave me a sense of virtuous purpose and orderly management of affairs—good things to bring away from N.D.G.; even a rational motive for having gone there in the first place.

Colds in the head are always more psycho than somatic, though, and mine was a present from N.D.G. that developed a day or two later out of a cross and melancholy mood that would not lift. No rhyme or reason to it. I had no intention of going back there. Truly had not the slightest wish to see Burt again. Just the same, I couldn't seem to get that damned housekeeper out of my head. Did she put enough salt in his morning porridge? Fold half the foot of his socks inside so he could get them on without help? And what had the bitch done with my plants? The thought of them pitched into some garbage can made me feel hot with resentment. And where had that idiot Johnny disappeared to? Surely he must be in hospital or jail. Nine days now he'd been totally invisible. Well, the ideal condition for that kind of man. Best for all concerned if he resigned from the universe. And the best of British luck to him.

In Sam's with a little pair of manicure scissors I'd found, I had to wait interminably for attention because it was Friday night and the place was crammed with noise, smoke, and people. Gloomily contemplated the bronze stag bearing off a naked girl on his antlers, the model of Bonsecours made entirely of toothpicks, the obsolete typewriters, cash registers, trombones, tripods that reduced the floor-space to a few narrow gangways. If I squatted down there, no doubt in time somebody would buy me. Meanwhile I sneezed and sneezed again. It was almost closing-time; pitch dark and very windy outside.

"Sam, what will you give me for these valuable scissors?"

Without a glance at me he put them close to his considerable nose. Profile like a Cretan tyrant full of rage, suspicion, and fear. He handed the scissors back carelessly.

"Five-and-dime. You keep them."

"Nonsense. That's silver-plate on the handles."

He had already turned away with a loupe in his eye to look at a ring.

"Sam, these are good scissors."

"All right, all right. Twenty-five cents."

"Fifty."

"Not on your life. A quarter."

"Oh, all right." What was the sense of arguing with the old skinflint? Little eyes like chips of mica. Who ever invented that myth fat men are all careless, good-natured fun-lovers?

Without speaking, he shoved a worn quarter into my hand and turned away to find his way blocked by his tall son. At once, in the glaring, fluorescent light, in all the noise and fug, his face was transformed; without a smile it lifted and opened in a look of love.

Something queasy squirmed all through me. I pushed off impatiently through the crowd and got outside with relief. The blustering wind set off a whole new train of sneezes and filled my eyes with tears as hot as coals. The way home, up the long hill, seemed three times as long as it was. Had to take

141

it slowly, because I felt so totally rotten. This must be flu. Nobody could suddenly feel so mouldy with just a cold.

The MacNab front door was heavy, and the wind shoved it so maliciously I could hardly have pushed my way in if someone hadn't just then pulled from inside. A figure in a low-pulled tuque and long overcoat, the collar pulled up all round. Johnny Horvath.

"For God's sake! Whatever happened to *you*?" I said. Because, although he at once turned sharply away to hide it, his face was a catastrophe—both eyes discoloured and his nose encased in some kind of splint-and-bandage affair.

"What on earth happened—were you hit on the head by a bus, or what?"

"Yes, I have an accident," he mumbled.

"Well, I wondered what had become of you."

"Better now," he said, keeping his face turned away. There was a hangdog air about him that irritated me fiercely. With as much cold dignity as I could muster (in view of the runny nose), I moved past him.

"Wait, please wait," he muttered.

"What for?"

"Eva, don't—you give me a cup of tea maybe? Cannot eat much yet because of loose teeth, but some tea—" How ugly his voice was, bubbling thick and nasal through the cast.

"No, I'll give you no tea," I said bluntly.

"Look, I just want to talk to you—"

"Well, I don't want to talk to you. Good-night."

That was dignified, I thought, and quite final. I went briskly to my own door and unlocked it. But he simply followed me down the stairs before I could close it again.

"*No*," I said.

"Just five minutes, to ask you something, Eva."

Impossible to stand there arguing and hissing at

142

him—the Coopers would be out any minute now to take ringside seats. "Make it short," I said, "because I have nothing I want to say to you."

But he refused to be kept on the stairs; herded me down and into the sitting-room, where he turned on lights and pulled forward the soft chair as if I were the guest.

"Five minutes," I said grimly.

"Only want to say one thing to you."

"Well, what is it?"

"Findlay says you give notice. You moving out."

"That's right."

"But why? No place as nice as this, we fix it up a bit. You don't want to move."

"Yes, I do. Now will you go. I'm not well."

"Me neither," he said mournfully.

"Good-night, then."

"But you won't refuse a cup of tea? Look, Eva—I stay away all this time because I'm ashamed to show you this face. Other things hurting too, like pride. And I knew you would be angry, despise me."

"And well you might be ashamed. You were drunk and got into a fight, didn't you?"

"Yes."

To avoid expanding on the subject, he nipped off to the kitchen and put on the kettle. I sat back heavily and blew my nose. Ah well, what was the point of talking about it? What earthly difference did it make anyway? In three weeks I'd be a mile away from here. Never lay eyes on him again, and a good thing too.

"Got my job back, you know," he informed me, setting out the cups.

"Oh. That's good."

"Yes; he apologize to me, I apologize to him. All okay now. I work well and hard, even like this."

"So the fight wasn't with Litvak."

He poured tea busily. "Where this place you thought of taking?"

"Never mind. And I have taken it."

"What a bad cold you have, dear Eva. Take this aspirin with your tea, you feel better." And he shook two pills out of a large bottle from his overcoat pocket.

The tea, very hot and sweet, was a comfort. I gulped the pills down.

"Truth is, you don't look much better than me," he said, as if that were a cheering thought. "Look, these shoes are wet, your two feet are cold as ice." Before I could stop him, he was on his knees, unlacing the shoes, pulling off my stockings, wrapping my legs in a blanket.

"You need somebody look after you."

A dry grin tugged my mouth crooked. "Think so, do you?"

He seemed amused at this too, and smiled, revealing a gap where two lower teeth used to be.

"What a brawl it must have been. Did the police pick you up?"

The smile disappeared abruptly. "Eva, I want to talk to you now, a serious talk. You won't leave here. Where you going to find a good place like this, lots of space, warm—I fix that door opens on the lane and you have your own entrance then, privacy. I get the MacNabs to pay for paint, we do up these rooms, why we'd be in heaven here, you and me."

"What! Now look here, Johnny—"

"Quiet till I finish. Now I have a lovely red rug just fit this room. Real Wilton carpet, like new. This fireplace here, you know it could burn coal or logs, keep us cosy all winter. I can fix this grate. I'm good with all kinds repair work, carpentry, can fix anything. You didn't know that. Can even make us a proper table for eating, and put some shelves each side here for all your books and mine—"

"No, Johnny."

"But I tell you, we would be in heaven here."

"We would be in cuckooland. Now get this clear.

144

You are not moving in with me. I am moving out in May. After that, you're welcome to the place, you and your rug both."

"How cold and hard you can be," he said quietly. He got up from the floor and took the empty cups to the kitchen, where he washed them. I lay back in the chair, feeling rather dizzy and tired beyond words. Opened my eyes a moment later to find him looming over me.

"I say good-night now," he announced with dignity through his bandaged nose.

"Good-night, Johnny."

"You will let me at least fix you the back door, save you coming in and out through the house, all those stairs. Just needs a bit of planing. I do it for you this week-end."

"Oh, really, there's no point in—"

"You let me do this small thing. Now go to sleep."

"Oh, all right."

He went off, still with that air of mournful dignity, as if I were the one in disgrace to be nobly forgiven. It would have made me giggle if I hadn't felt so miserable. As it was, I crawled into bed and dozed off at once, glad to forget him and everything else for a few hours.

So there went my privacy.

Sunday morning produced John H., complete with bandaged nose, paper bag, and a box of tools big enough to build the Ark. He proceeded at once to create an intolerable din and mess getting the door off its hinges. I longed to go out and escape it all, but I still felt wretched with my cold, and the moody grey sky had a look of rain. And at least he had the sense not to irritate me with his usual flood of chat. His mood was one of stately aloofness. Nothing to say, except to apologize once for the hammering.

But the place shook with it. Chips of dry old paint

whizzed through the air like bullets. Dust rose, and some rich Hungarian curses. The black tom leaped to the sill and stared in briefly, with astounded disapproval.

"Do the MacNabs know you're doing this?" I shouted.

"Of course."

"All right. I just wondered."

"Hinges very rusty, that's all. I get it soon."

But it was noon before he could work out the rusted pins and at last lay the heavy old door down full length on the floor. A flood of silvery light poured in, with a cool mineral smell of stone, earth, and water.

"Put on your coat," he said, "with that cold. It just take me a little while to plane it now."

But that, too, turned out to be a formidable understatement. Soon he had recourse to the paper bag, drew out of it a bottle of rye and a sandwich, and, sitting on the door as though it were a felled enemy, began a solitary lunch. He held up the bottle in invitation, but I said "No, thanks," very righteously, and went off to the kitchen to have my soup in solitary, huffy silence.

All afternoon he sweated over that door, wrestled it fiercely into one position and another, hacked its bottom with a saw and a plane, tried it on the hinges, and took it down again. At six o'clock, when the light began to thicken, he was still at it.

"Look, why don't you just forget it," I suggested. "That door must be a hundred years old. Just shove it back and forget it. What if it won't open? Nobody's come in here for generations and nobody really wants to. I'd just as soon it stayed shut, myself."

He gave me a hostile look. "I fix it if it take me all night."

"Please," I muttered.

"If you be kind enough to hold this end, I could manage better. Could ask Findlay if you too tired."

146

"No, don't bother the poor creature. Here—like this?"

"Yes. Careful, now, it's very heavy. Now we see . . ."

Two lean cats, friends or relatives of the tom's, looked curiously in at the proceedings and then scampered away again. We wrestled the door once more up on its hinges and tried it. It stuck. We took it down again. A star pricked out in the dusk. It was cold.

"Screwing thing," Johnny muttered, planing furiously. For all the cold air, his flannel shirt was patched with sweat.

"For pity's sake," I said at last, "unless you want pneumonia, give yourself a drink. Or else stick the thing back and forget it, which makes more sense, really."

"We both have a drink," he said. "You very pale. Sorry this turn out to be such a job. Here, take a big gulp, it warm you up."

After a whole second of hesitation, I accepted. Stooping to brace the heavy door had tired me out in just a few minutes. "That's right," he said cheerfully. "Don't you worry, we get the damn thing right yet, I fix the bugger." We had several medicinal doses from the bottle. Dark deepened and the air grew metallic with frost. It was full night-time when at last we tested the door on its hinges and it swung sweetly, clear of the floor.

"Aha," said Johnny, trying not to sound surprised. He opened the door wide in triumph, then shut it, pulling the latch to with a firm click. "Now you have a good, private door all your own."

"So I have. Thanks very much."

He held out the bottle. "Here; we may as well finish this. In glasses, maybe, now we not workmen any more."

It was profoundly good to sit down with my drink and wrap my coat close. The place was terribly cold. After a quick glance at me, Johnny poked his head into the fireplace and lit a series of matches to inspect the flue.

"Findlay tell me the chimney-sweep clean this one out with the others here last September, It would work fine now. Draught okay. Let's burn up some of this mess I make all over. I saw a few logs in the furnace place that time we have the flood. Kept them to dry. Hold on."

He gathered up the litter of newspapers, sawdust, wood chips, and paint flakes, and stuffed it all into the rusty grate squatting lop-sided on its three rusty legs. Nothing, you would think, could come of so much rubbish; but the blaze was lovely—quick, bright, and hot. I stretched out cold feet to it gratefully.

"Ah, that's better, eh?" demanded Johnny. He refilled our glasses and then went off to the furnace room, returning a moment later with an armful of dingy old logs.

"You see. They quite dry. We soon be warm."

After a certain amount of smoke and hissing, the fire prospered handsomely. It cast a glow of heat over us and made a shifting, fragile light, so pleasing that I turned on the lamp with reluctance. Johnny reached up coolly and turned it off again.

"You still mad at me?" he asked in his impeded voice.

"Oh, don't be silly." It struck me then that he might well misinterpret this, so I hastened to add, "Of course I'm not mad. Not in the least. What you do is none of my business. You have your life and I have mine. There's nothing to be 'mad' about."

"But you were. You still are. Please don't be mad at me any more."

"All right, if that will make you feel any better."

He sighed heavily. "You so difficult, Eva. You say you not mad in such an English voice I can tell you still mad. Well, if I tell you I'm sorry, then? You know how I feel about you. I'm crazy about you, it's the
148

truth. You know that. And you care about me, too. Or you not still be mad. Right?"

He brightened perceptibly at his own insight, and closed a big hand around my arm. I began to jerk it away, but saw that his day's work had left a raw scrape across the knuckles. "You'd better go home and scrub up now, or that will get infected."

His smile was broad and happy as a child's.

"Oh, Eva, you so funny. So female. I love you so much. Let me come and live here with you. We share the rent, eat well, I take care of all the food and do the cooking, and fix the place up for us—then the two of us have a home. Come, say yes. We would be in heaven here, you and me." Distantly, muffled by rain, the church bells bonged.

The rye and the cold and the fire among them had made me overwhelmingly sleepy. It took a huge effort to say, "Johnny."

"Yes, dear."

"Absolutely and finally, no. We are not going to live together. Here or anywhere. Got that?"

His hand was on my knee now, warm and heavy. The fire was like a drug. It was just too big an effort to argue any more. Oh, hell, maybe communication was an overrated art anyhow.

"But I stay here tonight," he whispered, his arms around me, and I couldn't be bothered to say no.

"What it is, you probably one of these Women's Liberals. Right?"

"What, those crazy bitches that hate having breasts? Not me. I like being female. As you should know."

"Then why don't you want to live together with a man? You want to be independent, be your own boss. In fact, you are a very bossy woman."

"Think so, do you?"

"I know it. Trouble is, you much too intelligent.

149

You don't trust the rest of yourself enough. Try to be reasonable all the time, is very bad for a woman."

"It's men like you that make Women's Lib. Well, I once wanted to get a Ph.D., but everybody agreed with you, so I never finished it. That should make you feel better."

"You minded that?"

"Yes, I did for a long time. Not now. Even then I had a hunch most Ph.D. research was no more use to the world than a cup of warm pee. Just the same—"

"You quite right. But with all your brains, why can't you see how good it would be, us living here together? Sharing everything? You haven't got enough money, you think I don't know that? But I earn well —could make you comfortable and take care of you."

"Oh, don't keep on about it, Johnny. I like living alone, and that's that."

"How long you been a widow, anyway?"

"I'm not a widow."

"Divorced, then?"

"Not exactly."

"Well, exactly what?"

"I've been separated from my husband since last fall. Look, I don't ask you a lot of questions—about that nose of yours, for instance—"

"Ah, last fall. That's when you come here first."

"Yes."

"Now I understand."

"Most unlikely."

"Yes, now I see."

"See what, I wonder."

"I always think it funny about you—somebody like you, coming to a place like this. And now I see it is because you never meant to stay. Always intend to go back to him. Am I right?"

"No, quite wrong."

"A quarrel; he was unfaithful maybe? You angry— too sore to go back right away. But soon you will."

"No. I never will. You've got it all wrong."

"I never will, too, but it's different with me. You see, I know my wife, Anna, has another man now. She still write me, but not often. Has not much to say to me any more. Twelve years is long. She don't have to explain—I know. So I could never go back now, even if the Communists weren't in Hungary. That's all gone. But you—you can just jump on a plane or a train and go back to him. When you say you leaving here in May, you really mean you go back to him, right?"

"Wrong."

"You really have rented another place?"

"Well, I haven't exactly signed a lease yet—but come to that, I never have here, either. But I put a deposit down for them to hold it for me."

"How much deposit?"

"Why do you want to know? Five dollars."

"That's all?"

"It was all I could spare. The woman seemed satisfied. Anyhow, it's all arranged. Her husband has a station-wagon; he's willing to take my things away for a dollar or two."

"Far from here?"

"Oh, a fair distance."

"Well, then, I move too. Move in with you."

"Oh no, you won't."

"Then I give you the five dollars and we forget all about moving. Look, you like me or not, Eva? You like that door I fix so you are private here? You like these shelves I build and the kitchen cupboard I fix up? And you like this that I do to you, and this; you know damn well you do. So why go away? All right, I stop asking to move in with you, if you really rather have it that way—even if it's crazy. At least it's not so crazy as you to move out altogether. This way I see you often, but you can still be a Women's Liberal. All right?"

"Johnny, I don't know. Have to think about it."

"You are not to think. Too much thinking—"

151

"I know. Ruins a woman. Move your leg, will you? Got a cramp."

"Tomorrow I fix that place in the bathroom floor. I know a fellow give me some tiles cheap. Then we paint it all a nice bright blue."

"White."

"Yes, bossy. Where does your husband live?"

"Never mind."

"But far from here?"

"Yes. Quite far."

"Not too far to go back, though?"

"Oh, shut up. I'm sleepy."

"Because I want you here. You know that. You happy with me, boss?"

"Go to sleep."

"Yes. In a minute. Tomorrow you phone and cancel the five dollars, yes?"

"I'll see."

"Promise now. Or else."

"Oh, all right. All right."

"That's right. Pretend to be cross, that way I know you really pleased. You funny woman. You lovely, big, warm, female woman, stay right here with me."

In another week, the sun began to warm the wet April air. Dark buds began to fatten on the stark trees, and a crocus or two here and there showed a rag of yellow or purple. We opened the door and all the windows to let out the reek of fresh paint, and the old black tom began to stroll in and out as if he owned the place. He inspected the newly blue bathroom and frowned. But he approved, it was soon clear, of Johnny, even going so far as to rub against his legs and speak to him in a rusty squawk.

"This is a terrible cat. Look at him—I never see so much dirt," said Johnny.

"Put him out, then. Of course he's horrible. Alive with fleas, too."

"Poor thing, we give him some meat. He can't afford to support even one flea. You like some nice meat, animal? Look, he has a sore eye, half shut, and such ears. You a prize-fighter then, cat? A dirty old wrestler? How you like a nice bath to make you clean?"

Gulping down hamburger, the cat replied to all this with hoarse bursts of purring, and blinked up a look at Johnny with his one yellow eye.

"You see, he would like a bath."

"You're never going to get that beast into a tub. Cats loathe being washed."

"No, no, he will like it. Make him feel great."

And he actually began to run water into one side of the deep kitchen wash-tubs.

"Johnny, I tell you, he'll fight like a tiger. Anyway, what's the point? All his friends are filthy. He likes being dirty. He lives outside, after all."

"But I think now he like to live with us. Look what a gentleman and so friendly. We make you clean, cat, you retire from fighting, and get nice and fat with us."

"Johnny, I don't *want*—"

"Now what's the matter—you don't like cats? This a very nice fellow, only a bit filthy. We make you clean, a good boy."

"You crazy man. He'll tear you to pieces if you try putting him in that tub."

But as usual, Johnny serenely ignored the voice of reason, and by appearing deaf made me wonder whether the dreary things that voice always had to say were worth hearing after all. Just the same, I fetched an odd pair of men's leather gloves from my collection and made Johnny wear them.

"I don't know what on earth you want to bother for," I grumbled. "All of a sudden you're like some respectable suburban mum. What's the matter, you afraid the neighbours will talk about your dirty cat?"

He gave me a look of hurt rebuke, and went right on assembling his shampoo and towels. As he tested

153

the water, the old cat circled his feet trustingly, still grinding out his laryngitic purr.

"Well, I'm going out for a walk. You clean up the mess, mind. And make sure you have some iodine handy; he's more of a fighter than you think. The two of you deserve each other."

I went off then for a cross stroll in the sun. For quite a while now, irritation had been building up like an itch about all sorts of little things Johnny did. He had insisted on buying the paint for the bathroom, and so, of course, it was now such a lurid blue that faces in the mirror looked hanged. He spent an entire evening making soup, and saturated the whole place with a disgusting smell of onions. Without a by your leave he poured bug-killer down the sink drain and all my old friends disappeared. Every day he proposed bringing down his red rug, and every day we argued about it all over again, until I lost my temper one night and suggested he do something anatomically impossible with his rug. At which he only spluttered out a mouthful of coffee, laughing. And now here he was, for God's sake, washing a cat in my kitchen sink!

Sunday was never my favourite day for walking, specially in bright weather. Too many church-going, respectable people about. Young lovers with linked fingers vaguely strolling, young couples pushing prams and tenderly guiding toddlers. Everybody with a place and secure in it. Everybody looking smug with content. It was no place for me in my beaten-up tennis shoes. I felt too hot in my thick coat. It was profoundly irritating to think I couldn't even go back to my own place of privacy. Finally I soothed myself by thinking of several outrageous things to say that would surely dislodge him for a while, and headed back home.

What a scene. The kitchen was wet, to put it mildly. Water glistened and dripped from the walls. Johnny was soaked. The shampoo bottle lay broken in a soapy puddle. Lurid scratches bled on Johnny's arms, and

154

the towels looked like tattered battle-flags. Shaking itself on the floor and looking furious was a wet, black weasel.

"Eva, is there a dry towel left? Must rub him or he'll die of a chill, poor old beauty." Down on his knees in the wet, Johnny bent over the weasel and rubbed it dry, talking to it all the time in a fatuous, loving voice. "See, he got a white shirt-front nobody knew was there. Was that nice, then, a nice clean cat. Get his lovely black coat dry he be a beauty boy. . . ."

Muttering I went into the other room to read. They both ignored me completely. Johnny continued to rub and blandish until a hoarse purr began to emerge from the towel.

A little while later Johnny called, "Eva! Come see our boy now."

"Idiot," I said. But I went in. There on the floor sat old tom, fluffed out to three times his old proportions by a coat of extravagant black fur. Amid all this the tattered stumps of his ears and his one good eye gave him the sheepish look of a tough old screw who has just been publicly saved. He smirked up at me, and in place of the old raucous croak uttered a pious little bleat. And Johnny looked at me with such pride—our child had said something clever—that I leaned against the sink and laughed till I was weak at the pair of them with their virtuous, questioning eyes.

On Saturday afternoons Johnny always listened to the opera broadcast. Not in his own place, as requested more than once; but in mine. On my FM radio. With the volume well up. Frequently singing along with the Wotans and Scarpias in a hearty, far-from-perfect bass. It was all a little less irritating than being pinched to death with sugar tongs, but not much.

"Can't you turn it down, at least!"

"It's not loud," he would shout. "Listen to this lovely bit. Ah, that poor Tosca."

"I would if you'd just shut up."

"La la la la la la—"

"Oh God, what's the use." So I threw open the lane door, dragged a kitchen chair outside with a box to prop my feet up, and sat down with a book under a hot yellow umbrella of sun. Just outside the door grew a huge ginkgo tree that gave a dapple of shade with its new silk leaves and provided a bit of welcome relief from the rows of decrepit fencing and battered garbage tins. There was even a patch of scuffed young grass doing its best just under the tree. A little May wind moved around, enjoying itself among the tall weeds. The sunlight came into my flesh like honey. Eyes closed, I saw the shape and colour of my own blood cells, pentacles and hexagons of burning red. Tosca's improbable dilemma faded into merciful remoteness. The breeze delicately stirred last year's dry leaves and tickled the stiff twigs of a derelict old lilac bush. Soothed, I thought, this is better than art, truer than religion, and began to doze off.

"Eh!"

Eyes jerked open. Instant irritation. A small and extravagantly filthy boy—surely one of the Leblanc children, though peeled out of his winter space-suit it was hard to be sure. Yes, it was. Running nose, tight, tilted eyes, and loose mouth. The retarded one.

"Eh," I said and closed my eyes again, hoping he'd take the hint.

A light whack on my knee soon took care of that hope. "Eh," he said again in his loud, toneless voice, and displayed a dirty stick. I eyed it and him with equal disfavour. His head was scruffy with dirt and hacked by a bad hair-cut, besides being too small for his swayback body with its strangely swollen belly. His feet flopped when he walked like fins. All in all, he was a botched job, like something put together out of a do-it-yourself kit. On top of everything else, he'd wet himself.

"Where's your mother?" I asked him in French.

A vacant stare past my eyes. Then he squatted down and whacked the ground near my feet with the stick.

"Why don't you go and find your mother?" I suggested loudly. He didn't look up. Deaf too, poor monster? He whacked away energetically, and one of the blows landed so near my foot I jerked it away sharply. At once he ducked almost flat to the ground, crowding his ear under one arm to shield as much of his head as possible. The speed and skill of that movement made me feel a qualm like nausea. I touched him on the shoulder and said "Wait here".

Among my found things was a painted windmill on wheels whose wooden spokes turned brightly when it was pulled along—had come across it in a park just the day before and thought it too amusing to leave there. I immersed briefly in the opera, found the toy, and brought it out to him.

"Here," I said. "Play with this."

He stared at it without comprehension.

"Look. Pull it along. Like this."

I demonstrated. The toy made a light clacking, and its chipped paint flashed. The child's wet, pink mouth gaped in a great grin of joy, and he grabbed the cord out of my hand. Down the lane he went on his flopping, clumsy feet, the clack after him arrested every few seconds because he couldn't run and look back simultaneously. I closed my eyes and invited the sun again. Dozed deliciously off.

"Eh."

Unwillingly yanked awake again as the windmill was pushed into my hand. It had not been improved by its trip down the muddy lane. The cord was tangled tightly around one of the wheels. I looked down at the strange, slanted eyes, clear blue as the sky. Not so retarded as all that, perhaps. Nor so ugly. There was something almost exotic about those eyes, with their look of primitive perception untainted by

157

intelligence or experience. His otherness had its own magic. In his cruel imperfection he reminded you what it was to be human.

I unwound the string and gave the toy back; he flopped rapidly off. After perhaps nineteen revisits, he learned how to keep the string free of the wheels. The sun dimmed gradually from gold to silver. I gathered up the unread book and my box footstool and opened the door to go in. The musical anguish of poor old Tosca must be over now. But there at my elbow was the child again, filthier than ever now, the windmill clutched to his wet front. He seemed to expect something more to happen, though I couldn't think what.

Resentfully, and touching him only gingerly, I guided him up the basement stairs and put him out in the hall. "Go up and find your mother," I told him. But he wouldn't climb up to the second floor. I had to clamber the whole way up with him, only to find when I knocked that no one was at home. The door was locked. Down we went again, to Mrs. MacNab.

"This child has been locked out. Where's his mother?"

"Oh, she goes down the street to a friend's for coffee sometimes—leaves him out to play when it's nice."

"A kid like this all alone for hours? Doesn't she know that trucks come down that lane?"

Mrs. MacNab's currant eyes rested briefly on the boy's smeared face without discernible pity, or even concern. "Oh well," she said, "his mother doesn't care much for this one, that's the truth. You can understand it, really. No business having kids at all, of course. They're living common-law, you know. She'll be back soon. Or the father will. I'll let him in upstairs. Come on, you. Just look at the mud you've tracked in here. My God, there's no end to it, the dirt those kids make. If he weren't so good with the rent, always on the dot, I'd put them all out tomorrow. Come on, boy."

But just before he dragged those guilty feet around the angle of the stairs, well ahead of Mrs. MacNab's prodding hand, he turned the dirty white moon of his face to look back at me.

With considerable relief I went below and thought about other things. A good situation to keep well clear of, that was sure. Just the same, I wondered what his name was, and what that crippled understanding made of "living common-law", and a mother who didn't like him.

That door, open now so often in the sunny, new-green weather, let in all sorts of intruders—not only the old tom, now an official resident, but a rag-tag of his tribe, for whom Johnny insisted on keeping a litter of food-saucers on the kitchen floor. A squirrel and a terrified rat were also among our callers. One dusk a bat blundered in for a look around, and Johnny lunged and fenced with it, armed with a spatula, his head swathed in a pink bath towel (bats get in your hair). I had the impression that the bat enjoyed the whole episode enormously.

All sorts of other things, less tangible, came in too, like the loud hilarity of the garbage collectors, a gang who found comedy a good answer to their profession. Floating crystals of dandelion fluff sailing on the spring air. Smells of car exhaust, chimes of bells, quarrels and laughter from upstairs windows. Neighbourhood kids paused, sucking thumbs, to stare candidly in. A Jehovah's Witness with the biggest Adam's apple ever seen called to urge immediate reform, because he had proof the world was about to end in flames. (I told him I was looking forward to it.) And of course Jean-Paul Leblanc flip-flopped in and out from time to time. Johnny occasionally brought in a friend or two for avalanches of chat, generally in French or Hungarian, with only shy smiles for interpreters. They were an odd lot, as surprising and various as Johnny himself. One was a philosophy professor from the Université de Montréal, one was a newspaper cub who reviewed concerts, another was a toothless little old Hungarian who worked with Johnny at the factory. It didn't bother them, or me either, that I rarely could follow any of their long, wrangling talks. The spring was making me soft, sleepy, with a mild, benign acceptance even of Johnny's most irritating ways. Sometimes I thought with a kind of wonder of those lost winter days of silence and privacy. It was strange to regret them so rarely now.

But one caller I was not prepared for; one early-morning visitor I did face with a sick drop of the heart. My husband Burt at the open door was another story altogether. I had been dozing and struggled to get up, all my flesh tight with dread and guilt. So here it was at last, the encounter I'd been dreading. His fair hair had gone almost white.

"Well, Eva."

"Yes, it's me all right. Do you want to come in?"

"Not much." He looked fastidiously around with his cold, pale eyes that observed everything, including a pair of Johnny's old slippers, the windmill lying on its side, and a bottle of rye on the floor by the bed. I tried again without success to stand up. But Burt had no face—it was blanked out like a touched-up photo, and with unspeakable relief I knew this was a dream and Johnny lay beside me in the dim room. The only thing was I couldn't seem to wake up.

"Well, you've been expecting me, haven't you?" he asked.

"Yes, in a way . . . how did you ever find this place?"

"Why did you leave me, Eva?"

"I don't know, really. Just couldn't see any point in staying, I guess. Not a good reason from your point of view, of course. I'm sorry about it, if that's any use."

It frightened me terribly that I couldn't wake up. At first he'd been cruelly stooped with his disease, leaning on a cane; but now he stood straight as a spear, his body as light and active as when we were first married.

"Why did you commit suicide?" he demanded. "Because that's what it amounted to."

"No, Burt, you're wrong. It's just the opposite."

"What I really want to ask you is this," he went on, without appearing to hear me, "and I think you owe me a plain answer."

"Yes. What is it?"

"Why, just tell me what *is* this all about? A bohunk workman in your bed. A drooling idiot on your lap."

"—that was only because he cut himself on a tin can—"

"But you've adopted him. You feed him."

"No, no, only a glass of milk or a few raisins. He's grossly undernourished. That's part of the—"

"You have a husband, a son, grandsons, and you left them for these two. *Why?* In the name of all that's sane, why?" Delicately he lifted his cane and poked the old cat, asleep on the end of the bed. It hissed at him and jumped away.

"What are your human obligations, Eva; to these freaks or to us, your own flesh and blood?"

"To everybody," I tried to say, but something closed my throat. His pale eyes looked at me with the cold, greedy lust I remembered so well. Labouring for breath I finally managed to get the words out: "Please forgive me."

At once his expression changed. His eyes were innocent now, as blank and pure as Jean-Paul's. When I took his hand, the flesh was cold as death; I longed to warm it.

"Oh, yes, I forgive—" he said, in a voice that

sounded almost absent-minded. "It's all past now. Do you want a divorce?"

"No, no, what would be the point of that?"

"You don't want to make a choice, you see. It's typical of you. Evasive. Never direct. Always over-subtle. But what about me? What about the neighbours?" His voice rose, thin with rage. "They pity me, and no wonder. While you live here with some-body else's mongoloid bastard, squandering—raving nonsense about obligations to everybody—" His pale flesh seemed to swell with a murderous anger. The air was tight and hot with it. I dared not move or say a word for fear of him. He made a slashing cut at the air with his cane; the sun flashed on it like steel, and I heard Jean-Paul's clumsy run, his blubber-ing wail of pain fading in the distance.

"Don't! Don't!" I shouted, and tried to catch his hands as they slashed with the glittering weapon. But what I really feared was that I might seize and use it to destroy him; it was my cane I'd found with the silver band. And Burt was weeping, the dry sobbing of years past for which there was no com-fort, no reparation.

"Eva! Eva!"

Blank, disoriented, my heart knocking, I looked into Johnny's face.

"You've been dreaming, a nightmare," he said. "Yelling 'Don't'—what the neighbours think I do to you?" He smoothed back my hair, damp with per-spiration. The cool blue light of early morning filled the room. The cat stretched and leaped up on the chair to sleep again. Birds were beginning to chatter at the window.

I closed my eyes. Yes, it was bad judgment ever to have opened that door.

For some time I'd almost forgotten that parks are

162

the true habitat of the dispossessed like me; but this morning I made straight for Lafontaine Park without even thinking about it. This was where the exiled, the displaced, the alienated, wandered under the sky or sat on benches with their silent faces turned up to the sun. This was where I belonged.

Some of the park regulars I recognized, like the stout old gent with the row of military medals pinned to his battered frock-coat, or the Negro woman who always dragged along a box on wheels loaded with the empty soft-drink bottles she retrieved from under bushes. He was a gentleman of leisure and read a newspaper through gold-rimmed spectacles; she was a business woman, hard and energetic; but they had the same look. Everyone who came to sit in the park had it: a look of experience completed. They were contemplatives; mystics. All a little crazy. Flocks of school-children hopping and fluttering to school used the park too; so did pretty office girls tapping to work, and mothers pushing strollers; but they all averted their eyes and hurried past us weirdly dressed dropouts. They couldn't afford to understand us, any more than we could afford to envy them.

There was a flash and glitter of sun as the wind drove gaps in the scudding grey clouds. Stiff clusters of new leaves shone green on the trees, whose limbs were black in the wet light. I found a bench and sat down heavily. The broken night and its dream had left me tired to the bones.

At the other end of the bench sat a tiny old woman dressed all in black. I'd seen her before, too, always in the same torn straw hat with cherries on it, and a trembling little chihuahua pressed against her black feet. Never spoke to her or anyone in the park before, but now something made me say, "Nice fresh day."

"It is," she said, with a courteous jerk of the hat. Her wizened face was as tiny as an infant's, but the

163

eyes, deep in blackened sockets, were as old as the race.

"You ever have dreams?" I asked abruptly.

The question didn't seem to surprise her. "Oh, yes. Everybody has. Mimi often has, don't you, love? Some people think God speaks to us in dreams."

"I hope they're wrong, then."

"Yours are bad ones?"

"One last night was. Terrible."

She made no comment except to murmur, "Mother's baby" to the shivering little dog.

"Life would be so much simpler without men in it —and it's the last straw, damn it, when they turn up to pester you in dreams."

"I dreamed I had Siamese twins once—boys."

"The thing is, for the first time, really, I see that I owe him an explanation. If that doesn't satisfy him, I'll have to go back. Even if I hate the idea. But I can't stand this—pity is worse than anger, worse than hate; it weakens you worse than death."

"Oh no, pity makes you strong. Very strong. I have four dogs—this little one I bring here alone, the others are too rough for her—but the social worker keeps on and on. You just can't afford to feed them, Mrs. Angelini, and yourself too. You are actually *starving* yourself; you just can't do it. You know that nagging voice they all have. But I can do it, you know. Easily. What do I need to eat? What I need is to feed them. She can't see that. The doctor is smarter. He gives me injections and a little pat behind, no arguments. Now he's a man. No, men are all right. Almost as good as dogs. Isn't that right, my sweet?"

"Quite right," I said, smiling. I took a deep breath of the cool, moist air. Some of the tight, apprehensive fatigue began to ease out of me.

"Well, it's something to have it settled, I suppose. I'll call my son today . . . then, if he really wants me

164

back, in spite of everything . . . just disappear will be best. Can't face a long wrangle with Johnny, that's sure. Rather not see Jean-Paul, either, poor brat. Better this way, he's getting attached to me." Vaguely I thought it odd of me to be talking like this to a stranger; but somehow I didn't think of her as a stranger.

"He's learned to say four words," I told her. "Just in a week or two. One ear is quite good; it's just the other . . . of course his mother never talks to him, that's partly why he never . . . Johnny says she was brought up in a convent. The kid has two religious medals around his neck. God, aren't people queer? No wonder the whole planet's such a mess. Poor old God sitting up there; he's given up. All he can do is groan and laugh and hit himself on the forehead to think what he started. Well, I suppose I'd better find a dime and a phone booth to call Neil. *Won't* he be pleased to welcome the prodigal back! I just hope the fatted calf doesn't choke me. But I'll be all right, as soon as I get settled down and used to the bars. Burt was so devastatingly right. How free am I now —with that ever-talking John around all the time and the boy day-times—it's been a pleasure to talk to you, Mrs. Angelini."

She looked up from the dog with a frown—she had forgotten I was there. But then she made a gracious little bow with the broken hat, and said "God bless you."

I trotted briskly along the path with its trembling green puddles. Crushed red cat-tails from the budding trees made a rich smell in the cool air. I felt light and warm with relief. It was over at last, this exile. The dream had been painful and terrible, but curative as an amputation. Now there was no choice.

Still, now the whole thing was finally settled, it occurred to me there was no need to rush. It was barely nine; Neil wouldn't be at his office yet. There was time for a leisurely stroll; maybe even time to do one last bit of finding. Parks were generally not good hunting-ground, though, for anything but torn newspaper or kids' balls. Still, I might just come across something for Jean-Paul. Be nice to leave him some little thing.

For quite a while, no luck; only the broken head of a rubber doll. Then, at last, under a deserted bench, I spotted a little red truck. With that bright colour it would make the big mouth spread in one of his rare, wide smiles of joy. Squatting down I made a long arm and dragged the toy out; stayed there scraping it clean of mud until two giggling teen-agers went by, poking each other.

"All right, kids," I thought without resentment. "You're too young yet to know anything about finding. What I find is mine and everybody's; it belongs to anyone, like the sky, and it's worth having because of that, even if you might call it garbage—it's worth having just because I've found it. Not been given it, or bought it, but found it. Oh well, you have to be a dotty old creature living underground to know that. Friend and even relative of bugs and idiots and Hungarians and Mrs. Angelini. May I never forget this in N.D.G. Because it's an important truth, isn't it, darling?" And I began to giggle, still squatting there on the ground with my little truck, to think of all this wisdom and what on earth I would do with it back on Old Orchard Street. Then I got up and went along to find a phone booth and call Neil before that last thought could sober me up too much.

"—sorry, Mr. Carroll is out of town and won't be back till noon on Monday. Can I help you, perhaps?"

"No, you can't . . . to put it mildly. But thanks for asking. I'll call another time."

"Would you like to leave a message?"

"Just say his mother called. And will call again for sure on Monday, if she can hold on to her good intentions."

166

"I'll see he gets the message," the voice trilled. "Have a nice week-end, Mrs. Carroll."

In that vehement way it has, the Montreal spring rushed into hot summer-time overnight. By Monday the air was languid with heat; leaves everywhere had opened lavishly, and a white sun glared on the dry sidewalks. Even in a light dress I felt breathless walking down the hill to make my call, my feet hot in the tennis shoes. Even my eyes felt hot behind the big tinted glasses. I left the door of the phone booth a little open for air and dialled the number slowly, wishing I didn't feel so drugged and languid. This aftermath of a vigorous night with Johnny was not, I well knew, the proper condition at all for announcing a noble decision.

"Well, Neil, you got back all right."

"How are you, Mother? Yes, the plane was even on time, for a change. Everything all right with you?"

"Yes, dear, fine. But I called, actually, to tell you—"

"Look, I'm really glad you called. The fact is, I've been thinking a lot about you lately—I mean, more than usual. Now back there last fall, you asked me very reasonably to send along some of your own things from the house—clothes, and your jewellery, and so on. And I was so involved with Dad and his problems I never did what you asked. It must have annoyed you plenty. So before I left town last week-end, I packed up two big suitcases full of your things —all your shoes, coats, your dresser-set, things like that. Now just tell me how to get it to you, and I'll—"

"Neil, I don't need any of that now. The fact is—"

"If you'd only call me more often, Mum—we get so out of touch—surely you want your things."

"No, I don't. Tell me, how is your father these days?"

"Well, that's one of the things—I mean, for several
167

weeks now, he's been considerably better. Surprisingly better, in fact."

A sort of attentiveness woke up in my sleepy flesh. What was it in Neil's voice—a sort of embarrassment?—but I hadn't told him yet what I meant to do.

"Better, is he? Well, that's good. I suppose it's the warm weather helping at last."

"Er—yes. And he's much more cheerful."

"Is he."

Neil paused and I waited. Then we both spoke together. "It's quite a change. He actually goes out now for little rides. . . ."

"Because I've been doing a lot of thinking, and it seems to me I should at least discuss with him—"

"What was that, Mum?"

"Sorry, Neil. You were saying he goes out now."

"Yes, just for little drives when it's nice. With Mrs. Pratt. And the dog."

"Does he."

"And he's talking about having a patio built in the garden this summer. For outdoor meals."

"Really?"

"Yes. It's quite amazing, he's walking and moving around so much better. Sleeping well. A terrific change from what it was like even a month ago."

"Is it really."

"But Mum, what about you? Have you been all right?"

"I've been great."

"Your voice sounds funny. Is it the line, or have you got a cold or something?"

"Something sticking in my throat."

"Now, Mum, about these suitcases. I can send them along to you today if you'll—"

"No, don't bother, Neil. There's really nothing there that I want any more. Forget it. Thanks anyway."

"Well, but listen, Mother. I haven't forgotten, either, that months ago you mentioned a separation allowance. At that point, though, I couldn't get anywhere with Dad. But just recently I hinted again I thought he ought to do something like that, and while he didn't exactly say anything, I got the impression he actually might agree to some kind of regular arrangment one of these days. I'm going to bring it up again next time I see him, anyhow. After all, you need—"

"No, no. Neil, I mean this: I wouldn't accept anything from him now. Don't bring the subject up again."

"But Mum—look here, you're not sore at me about it, are you? I know I've been—"

"No, my dear, of course I'm not. But do as I say and just forget about the money. I don't want it. And I'm not sore at anybody. Not Burt, or you; certainly not Mrs. Pratt, or even the dog. Of course I should have kept in touch with you more. I'm a bit sore at myself, that's all. Imagine having an out-of-date nightmare. Bad scene, as they say. It's not what you decide, it's how you time it, I guess, which is a very deflating thought."

"I don't follow you, Mum."

"No, thank God."

"Look, didn't you start out by saying you had something or other to tell me?—What was it?"

"Nothing important, dear. How are things at home? The boys all right? And how is Kim?"

"She burns incense in her room."

"Well, don't sound so glum about it. You're lucky, the way some kids are, she's not burning the city down. Cheer it up. Don't be depressed about me, either. I'm all right. Just fine, in fact."

"You always say that. But is it true?"

"Of course it is."

"I often wonder what your life is like now, Mum, wherever you are."

A kind of peace crept into me at the familiar sound of love in his voice, as if at last something of
169

value was being communicated in spite of our clumsy words. Indeed, the dialogue we were actually having jogged to and fro with a clown's absurdity that struck me as almost too funny to endure.

"I keep busy," I said. "Planning a bit of house-cleaning. The time goes." (Yes; Johnny's mouth on my flesh. Wiping Jean-Paul's nose.)

"That's good. I suppose by now you've probably made a few new friends."

"Yes, quite a few." (The toothless Hungarian, the Spinoza professor. Mrs. Angelini and Mother's Darling. Myself.)

"That's good."

I smiled. "And a little hobby gets me out. Oh, I'm fine."

"It's so good to hear that. Do call me more often, Mum. I hate being out of touch; it worries me."

"I'll call every week. How's that?"

"Great. That's a promise, now. Next Monday, for sure." Relief in his voice. Was he as glad as I was to end this ridiculous, hearty exchange of clichés?

"For sure. Love to Kim. Au revoir, dear."

Before leaving the phone booth, I paused to count my money. Luckily, I had some to count. There was no liquor at home, and if ever a time was at hand for buying a large bottle of something intoxicating, this was it. After flipping the dime chute and collecting my own ten cents as a bonus, I headed down the hill briskly for the nearest grog shop. It's not every day you offer to sacrifice your life, after all, only to find that nobody's interested. Embarrassment like that can be quite traumatic. If Juliet had stopped Romeo's dagger hand to say, "Don't be a nit, dear," or St. Theresa had heard God say, "No, thanks, duck," they would have understood exactly how I felt, and how necessary this bottle was.

"Is that you, Johnny? Come on in . . . I want to talk to
170

you. I mean a serious talk—and keep those damn cats out."

Too late. Four or five of them were already pouring in around his legs, and he made no more than a half-hearted attempt to dam the flood. Before coming in he paused to take off his shoes and pour himself a cold beer, talking through from the kitchen.

"Hot as boiling out there, but so lovely and cool down here. I see that poor bitch Jeanne on the street —she look big enough for twins. When she due, anyhow? You know if she have a girl—"

"Yes, I know. Those wretched brats of hers will be worse off than ever. Are you coming in here? I want to—"

"No, it will be good then. She won't care, even more. Jean-Paul be more with us."

"Oh, great. Now that's part of what I want to—"

"What you think, Bill on the *Journée* give me two tickets for the second Rubinstein concert next week. You like to go? Oh, you having a drink, Eva? That's good. Buy a new bottle, welll"

"You'd better finish your beer. You're not going to like this much. And put your shoes back on."

He was already in a chair, plunging to and fro in a large, dilapidated book. "Listen, now, Eva, I get this from the library, here is mentioned Glanville, Oxford scholar and Royal Society man, and he believe, like me, in witches. What's more, listen to him say this: 'Most of the looser Gentry and small pretenders to Philosophy and Wit are generally deriders of the belief of Witches and Apparitions.' Now how about that?"

"Hasn't Glanville been dead about three hundred years? But never mind that. The thing is, Johnny, I've decided I need more—bip—more privacy. You're around here far too much. It's got to stop, or else I'll have to move out. I mean, it's ridiculous, people and cats underfoot all the time, and all this damn singing, talking, cooking, arguing that goes on. I never get a

171

minute's peace. And that's not what I came for. I walked out on all that domestic stuff. Spinet desk and people hanging on. You understand, don't you?"

"Sure," he said comfortably. "Eva, darling, you been home how long drinking out of the new bottle? Your face kind of pink."

"Never you mind my face. Do you get the message? It is just plain ridiculous for you to practically live down here, and it's got to stop right away. I like you and all that, as you know; but after all, you have your own place to—bip—go to. So will you go there. I'll maybe ask you down for a meal once in a while, but not often, if you don't mind. Got a great many things of my own to do and think about." Relieved to have that over with, I finished off my drink. All the ice-cubes in it rushed down and tapped my nose smartly.

"That's all right," Johnny said easily, stretching out his legs.

"Well, then—bip—you might as well go now." And by way of setting an example, I heaved myself up out of the deep chair. The room immediately swelled around me and shifted in a very curious way, like stage scenery in a draught. The heat, no doubt.

"And when you go, please push all those cats out."

His smile was almost tender with affectionate amusement. "Look, darling, I make you some nice strong coffee first."

"Don't re bidiculous, I don't want any coffee. Just go. And stay away till you hear from me."

Obligingly he drained off his beer and stood up. "Okay, you say go, so I go. Why don't you lie down for a little bit." He thrust his feet into the shoes and added with a cheerful grin, "That way maybe you not feel too bad in the morning." With that he took himself off, still grinning.

When the door was safely closed, I sat down again—or, rather, allowed the chair to reach up and repossess me. Raising my glass, I drank to my own good management, promptness, tact, efficiency, and wisdom. He hadn't made a row. He had no hard feelings. He and the cats would from now on pay only an occasional, dignified call, and for the rest of the time I would live in blessed peace.

"Here's to—bip—privacy," I said. "Here's to me. Alone in paradise at last."

Very soon after that, I did lie down, and at once, precipitately, went to sleep.

In the morning, though I woke rather late, I felt magnificent. There was so little left in the whiskey bottle, I concluded Johnny must have spilled some somehow, before he left. Clumsy brute.

It was a beautiful day, clear and big with wind. I decided to take myself on a long excursion, right up to the park on top of Montreal, where high on the rough green hill you could look down over the whole smouldering, humming city below. On a day like this you could see far across the bright river and over the American border to the faint blue of the Vermont mountains.

I could have hugged myself with happiness once I got up there in all that lovely space. There wasn't a soul around. Nobody came up here on week-day mornings. The city spread out below was just a distant mutter and growl. It was so quiet all around, you could hear the birds talking and hear the wind rushing around playing in the leaves.

The sun was like a broad, warm hand on my back as I started to explore the beaten earth paths. With my cane I prodded and lifted the skirts of bush after bush, looking for things; and before the afternoon was half over, I'd found a real prize—a man's good English mackintosh, lined in red tartan, not so much as a button missing. Fancy losing a thing like that. She must have said no at the last minute—or laughed at the wrong one. Of course, it was a bit grubby and crumpled, but a good wash would take care of that. And it wasn't much too big for me. Spring-coat problem solved. I was so pleased I couldn't stop smiling, and by mistake even smiled at the bored policeman strolling by, who gave me a hard stare in return, as if a smile were illegal.

The sun and wind up there felt so good I stayed all afternoon. Eventually I found a bench and had a little snooze. By the time I made my way home through the tangle of evening traffic, I was hungry and leg-weary, and my arm ached with the weight of the shopping-bag I took on all my finding trips. In it were the coat, a skipping-rope with red handles, a wool headsquare, a kid's lunchbox with Superman on it, and a rain-bloated guidebook to the Riviera.

My place was blessedly empty and quiet. I heard some cats yelling to get in at the door, and said happily to them, "Go to hell." I climbed into bed with two hard-boiled eggs for supper, and ate them while I read the guidebook. Soon I fell into a child's deep sleep.

Next morning, just outside the lane door, I found one of Jean-Paul's bruised and swollen little shoes. His mother was quite capable of sending him out to play barefoot among the broken glass, or, alternatively, of keeping him locked in out of the sun for the rest of the week. So I went upstairs and knocked at their door to hand it in. Rather to my surprise, Jeanne's sallow face offered a faint smile.

"Well, thanks, I looked everywhere for this damn shoe, you know what he is, he won't keep them on, I don't know what to do with him. Come on in, I got coffee hot."

She urged me in so briskly I had no real choice. Politely concealing reluctance, I sat down, after finding a place to prop my shopping-bag.

174

The room was arranged around an enormous TV set on long metal legs. Everything else in the place had a look of irrelevance, right down to the two kids squatting in a corner watching an unnaturally muscular young man on the screen doing exercises with terrible energy and good cheer. Jeanne poured hot water onto coffee powder at a round table littered with dirty dishes, a roll of toilet paper, six full ashtrays, thumbed copies of *'Allo Police* and *Movie Mirror*, playing cards, a patent-leather poodle, a jar of cold cream, and a child's torn shirt. There was a tin of peas in the fireplace (twin of mine downstairs), and a chamber pot on the mantelpiece beside a tinted picture of Pope John XXIII.

After giving the cups a casual stir with a fork-handle, my hostess lit a cigarette and settled back for a chat.

"The kids both got some kind of rash, maybe the heat we had lately. My God, it was hot enough up here to fry eggs on the floor the other day." She spoke English easily, but she had a flat, toneless voice, the kind of voice women keep for telling you they have a headache. She didn't look at the children, but I did. Jean-Paul sat with legs straight out in front of him, a once-pink pacifier in his mouth and his face slimy with tears. The other boy was impassively eating potato chips out of a large bag.

"How old are they—about five and three? Mine used to take off his clothes, shoes—everything—at that age whenever he could. Took his pants off in church, once."

She eyed me curiously through a cloud of smoke.

"How many kids did you have?"

"Only one."

"You were lucky." With a hand to the small of her back she shifted her bulk in the chair.

"When is the new baby due?"

"The end of June."

"I suppose you hope for a girl this time."

To my surprise, this commonplace remark woke her pale, heavy face into some kind of animation.

"Oh, yes, I'm crazy to have a girl. Always wanted one. This one has to be a girl. Look, I'll show you what I got ready—" Shoving the older boy aside as if he were a chair, she opened the drawer of a near-by bureau and carefully drew out two frilly little dresses of cheap, sheer nylon in candy colours of pink and green. There were matching bonnets, also frilled, and a tiny white plastic purse with a kitten on it.

"Cute," I said helplessly.

"Yeah. I always wanted a girl."

"Well, sons are pretty good too." After a second's hesitation, I took a plunge. "Look, I know you have a problem with Jean-Paul; but, you know, he plays around the lane a lot these days, and I've got to know him . . . he's a nice little fellow . . . you won't mind if an old grandmother like me makes a suggestion? If a doctor could go over him completely, I think quite a lot might be done to help—you know, little things, like if the adenoids came out he might not get so many colds—and with a hearing-aid— there's only one ear that's—"

But her face had closed in such a sulky and final way that my voice trailed away. However, having gone this far, I was stubborn enough to finish.

"—places like the Children's Hospital have such good clinics now. They could evaluate him there, make tests and so on, and I think they might be able to do a lot for him. He has quite a lot of potential, actually."

"No, I don't believe in them snooty English doctors," she said flatly. "I take him anywhere, it'll be to put him in St. Jean de Dieu; that's the place for kids like him."

The coffee turned sour in my mouth at the thought of Jean-Paul in that great grey city barrack where thousands of the retarded and disturbed live as the dead live. I levered myself up and collected my bag. "Well, thanks; I'd better be—"

Jeanne turned away and, with impersonal accuracy, smacked away her older boy's hand from his genitals. She ignored his other hand, which was picking his nose. Before opening the door for me she lit another cigarette.

"I see Johnny working around your place a lot lately," she said, her eyes sliding over me curiously.

"Oh, he's quite a carpenter. Likes to help out the MacNabs by doing little repairs for them, now Findlay isn't well."

"He does it for you, you mean. Marc and I figure it's quite a romance." A sly smile narrowed her lips.

"I'm a long way past the age for romance," I said, moving closer to the door. But she was persistent; malice brightened her eyes and curved her lips so she looked almost pretty.

"Oh, but Johnny's quite a Romeo, you know. Didn't you know that? He's a bad boy, a real sex-pot. He even tried to get funny with me; I had to tell my husband to quit asking him around. And of course you heard about the awful fight he got into over that waitress, her boy friend broke his nose for him, that slowed him down for a while, but I'll bet you these days he's—"

"Sorry, but I really have to go now. Thanks for the coffee. See you again some time. Au revoir, Jean-Paul." Trying not to seem in too big a hurry, I finally escaped from the reek of smoke and grease and dirty child in the place; but it clung in my clothes and hair for hours afterward. It was a relief to get out and about my finding, and put the whole conversation out of my mind. None of it, after all, had anything to do with me.

But that evening as soon as I opened the door, I heard sizzling in the kitchen and smelled chops frying. Johnny's curly head showed around the door, and he waved a stick of French bread in genial greeting.

"What the hell are *you* doing here?"

"I make dinner for you. Nice pork chops. You like that."

"Johnny, I told you to stay away."

"But I did stay away. Last night I stay away. Very lonely. But I figure you probably have a pretty big head yesterday, I leave you alone with it."

Too tired, and disliked the feeling of irritation too much, to argue with him. "You are leaving immediately after dinner. I want an early night. And leave me your key, what's more."

Much clattering in the kitchen. He was determined not to hear me. I opened the door and pulled out my chair and box for a calming sit under the ginkgo. The evening sun was still warm.

For once the lane was empty of shrieking kids. Nobody around but a skinny old man, bent over in the narrow strip of earth behind the next-door house. He had a little row of flowers there, tall red tulips like grenadiers burning and brilliant among all the dust and litter. The man himself had a face like a raisin, dry, small, and wrinkled; and red, bad-tempered little eyes. He dug and weeded his little bed with a sour, critical air, like someone keeping unruly children in order by threats. On impulse, and to keep my mind off Johnny, I said, "Nice little garden you have there."

He straightened up in instalments and fixed me with a frowning eye. "Tulips are fair this year, pretty fair. The daffs didn't amount to much, though. I had the only ones on the block. It's all knowing how to store your bulbs. Now you take—"

And off he went on a long, dull lecture I made no effort at all to follow. Plenty of practice in my life at the gentle art of enduring male monologues on subjects like hockey, balance of trade, and such things.

178

You just throw an occasional "Oh, really?" or "Of course" into the rare pauses and look vaguely benign. They never know. In this case, I was even rewarded by a small bouquet of three tulips presented over the fence with a rusty smile.

It had grown chilly, so I took them in.

"Look, aren't these nice?—like cool fire."

He scowled at them as if they offended him.

"Why you been out there so long—you waiting till I go, or what? You can't stay in the same room with me even an hour? I'm just here to cook, put out the meal like a waiter or what?"

"Calm down, I just wanted a bit of air. It's stuffy in here."

"And who's that old bugger you talk to, anyhow?"

"Johnny, I don't know his name. Now don't annoy me."

"You pick him up next, I suppose."

"Oh, will you cut it out."

I put the tulips into water, and he took a swallow from a rather dark drink.

"That guy next door has a big sow of a wife. She drinks all day and they fight like two animals, you'll hear them in the summer plenty if you haven't already. He'll be after you, with his flowers. And you would flirt even with a corpse like that."

"Johnny—"

"Yes, well, you sit out there grinning at him—"

It was too much. "Well, you're a fine one to come all over righteous, aren't you?—you and your waitress."

At once he blushed crimson, a ridiculous sight that irritated me more fiercely than ever.

"Who tell you that?" he muttered.

"So it's true, then? It was her boy friend who broke your nose? You never told me that little detail."

"But who tell you?—not Findlay."

"Jeanne Leblanc, if it matters. She seems to know a lot about you. Says you even made a pass at her."

He took another gulp of his drink, and said hastily, "Well, I never did. She only wish I would, that Jeanne. Why do you listen to dirty gossip from somebody like that?"

"It's true, isn't it?"

"Look, would you like to know what people say about you? They say you shoplift, coming home every day with that big bag. How you like that for gossip?"

"I said, it's true, isn't it?"

"Yes, well, don't get sore about an old story. I just— well anyhow, it's all over with her since two weeks ago, so forget it. Let's have some dinner."

"Two *weeks* ago!"

"Quietly, Eva—"

"Do you mean to tell me that all this spring when you were down here every spare minute talking about living in heaven here you were bedding some bitch of a girl?"

My language appeared to shock him a good deal, but by now I was too exalted with rage to think that amusing.

"Now you just get yourself out of here, lover boy," I went on, without troubling to lower my voice. "And don't try coming back, unless you want me to call the police."

"Yes, all right, I'm going," he said. But he crumpled onto the kitchen stool and took another swallow from his glass as if he felt ill. He looked ill; he looked drained and middle-aged and very tired.

"I wish you could understand how it was," he said. "She such a pretty thing, just twenty, part Indian with a French mother, those black narrow eyes; so pretty, and a whore. All the time I have her and think this is my girl, I'm not so old and funny-talking, with no home—all the time she was sleeping with a big ape works at that nightclub, you know the one near the bus depot. It was him broke my face up, the big meatball. You see, I never knew she had him too. But even then, after we have this big fight, I couldn't let

180

her go, she sleep with me a few times, but soon I see she is only doing it because she felt sorry for me a bit. And because she is a whore. So I left her. That's over now. All finished. You see, I've been so lonely for a long time. That's why I come to you this winter, that's why I ask you to live with me. It's the honest truth. I never told you any lies. Never."

"Just get out," I said. The rage was gone. Nothing left now but a freezing anger and the taste of metal in my mouth. "And leave me that key."

He looked at me briefly and then got up without saying any more. He laid the key on the kitchen table. The door closed behind him with a quiet click.

The next day, of course, was Sunday. It always is after anything disagreeable has happened. A torrid day, white sky glaring, the motionless air stretched tight as silk with heat. I spent the morning tidying up—the sitting-room had somehow accumulated tons of dishevelled newspaper, full ashtrays, toys, empty bottles, stray magazines, and other litter. It gave me a grim satisfaction to stuff load after load of this junk into paper bags and cram them all into the big garbage tin behind the house.

"Well, that's that," I said to myself. "Now I can get on with my life." Among the things I threw away was a torn sheet of cheap paper on which Johnny had painted a picture in bright poster-paints to amuse Jean-Paul. There was a red house perched crookedly on a yellow hill; in the bright green sky a big white bird flew. The colours were so gay and clear I hesitated a second before crumpling it up; but then I shot it in ruthlessly with the rest of the garbage. Picked up, washed, and put away with finality all the saucers of cat-food. When I'd finished all this, the apartment looked neat and suitably grateful, and I sat down to enjoy a genuine sense of virtue.

Not the least, by any means, of my victories was

181

refusing to let myself relive or discuss mentally a single detail of yesterday's parting row with Johnny. It was over; that was the end of it all; there was no more to be said. All night I had been in a fever of anger; that was gone now, too, and I was as calm as stone.

The only problem with this kind of self-approval is deciding what to do with it. Blandly the neat apartment looked at me. Church bells shooed the last of the dutiful to late mass. Feet scuffed and tapped along the pavement in response. I wanted to go out; but where? What to do with my hard-won solitude and leisure? Because they were hard won. I knew what rejecting Johnny meant, I knew being without him was going to be lonely and hard. That only increased my certainty I'd done the right and proper thing. I'd been true to my own principles at last. It was a real achievement, and it seemed to me to justify sending off a modest message—

"Sir, with respect, being in a state of grace may not be much fun, but it's gratifying, and it's a change You're sure to approve. At least from now on I'll be doing what was originally intended—living austerely alone, taking and giving nothing, just doing my finding trips, and thinking, and being. That was what I asked for in the beginning, all I asked for or needed.

"I really owe You an apology, in fact, for these last months and their impure intentions and mixed-up hesitations. Much more reprehensible, these, than leaving Burt was. That had some justification, or at least some dignity. Anyhow, I'm sorry about all the rest of it, and intend to sin no more. Your friend, Eva."

Nice to be reconciled at last. Oh, it was good to be at peace and alone with myself. I drew a long sigh of contentment. What would I do with my day? Just walk a while, perhaps; Sunday was hopeless for finding, but not bad for looking at people and things generally. I left the bag at home, but took my trusty cane and set out early in the afternoon.

182

The park was a place to avoid—on week-ends you stepped over interlocked couples wall to wall, as it were. But walking on the pavements soon burned my feet. For a moment I was almost tempted to climb steps and go up into the cool darkness of a cathedral whose open doors sent out a rustle and murmur of multiple praying—but I didn't really feel quite regenerate enough for that. Anyhow, as Johnny once said, with his usual air of pronouncement, the only prayers worth hearing are silent.

Heat like a monstrous glass bell pressed down over the city. Everywhere clusters of people leaned out of windows, fanned themselves on narrow balconies, or sat on the street in a surprised-looking assortment of chairs. Always together. Never anyone alone.

Vaguely thinking an air-cooled movie might be a good idea, I trudged in the blaze up the hill to Ste. Catherine Street. Johnny had been buying all the food for quite a while, so I actually had folding money left over from last month's cheque and could well afford the ticket. But all the local theatre had to offer was some horribly amplified slop, called *The Sound of Music*, gusting out of the swing-doors. No, thanks, I'd had enough of that kind of thing.

It might have been pleasant to go along and look quietly at pictures in the Museum, but my dirty old tennis shoes put that out of the question for today. For ever, come to that. I'd got used to these shoes now; even developed a kind of loyalty to them. And that barred me, perhaps permanently, from pretty well every public place in the "nice" west end of town. This I no longer regretted or resented at all. I only wished strongly that libraries and junk shops and used-book stores—interesting places like that—would stay open on Sundays.

Eventually I took a long bus ride around the green crown of town. Cruising along the tree-lined streets of Outremont gradually fanned a little coolness into my cheeks. The leisurely, ponderous rock of the bus

183

was soothing. I felt serene and good. No resentment against a living soul. A young girl lifting her hand to a flutter of long hair made me think briefly, with love, of Kim. As the bus plunged downhill toward home, I thought with compassion and even a twinge of affection about Burt, sunning his poor bones on the new patio with his dog and his widow. I even thought with momentary pity of Johnny's violent, sordid passion for the narrow eyes of his Indian girl. All that sour, burning anger of yesterday and last night was gone. (Except that the bastard might have been honest with me from the start.) Hastily I got off the bus and walked the last ten blocks at a brisk pace, till the heat dragged me to a crawl.

Well, anyhow, I had no fear now that he would come around, knock at the door, or in any way make a nuisance of himself. After the merciless things I'd said to him, he would never bother me again. There was something primitive, even innocent, about his attachments: they were all or nothing. But there was nothing simple about the man himself. Under all his effrontery and bounce, he was a painfully proud man, with deep sadness under his surface gaiety. It hadn't been hard to destroy him.

Not, of course, that I'd done any such thing. Only preserved myself. Silly, inflated way to think of it. Not worth thinking about at all.

Once inside my own quiet, tidy room, I sat down with a deep breath of satisfaction. Down in the harbour a ship's horn hooted into the motionless air. I stretched out my legs and sighed again. Didn't feel like reading much. Not hungry. No sense sitting outdoors in the heat. Nothing to listen to on the radio but gloomy panels on pollution or adenoidal lectures on the Middle East crisis. Nothing to do. Not thirsty. Not hungry.

For a long time I sat there just looking in front of me, not thinking about anything in particular. Not feeling either sad or happy. It slowly grew dark. I wasn't hungry. There was nothing I wanted.

The white heat paralysed everything, even time. For days on end the sun glared, the still air blazed; all through the endless nights not a breath stirred the leaves.

I stayed indoors in my darkened room, fanning myself, and there was no real difference between the hours of day or night. Vaguely I held a book sometimes, or drifted into a heavy, unrefreshing doze. It was like waiting for some interminably delayed train or some incredibly dilatory dentist, except that I was waiting for nothing and nobody.

Early one morning, though, I woke to hear some kind of commotion going on overhead, and climbed laboriously up the basement stairs to unlock the door and see what was wrong. In the hall Findlay and his mother, the taxi-driver from upstairs, Marc Leblanc in an undershirt, and Mrs. Cooper fully dressed were all standing around while two men in uniform lifted and tilted a stretcher, trying to get it and its strapped burden out through the front door.

"Wait," Findlay said. "Someone give a hand here and I'll prop this side of the door open. That's it."

"Mind the paint," said Mrs. MacNab.

"Who is it?" I asked.

"My husband," said Mrs. Cooper.

"Oh . . . going to hospital? I'm sorry."

"No. He died this morning, just before light."

I glanced at her. She was calm, in the merciful novocaine of shock, but her face was paper-white, and there was a strange little perpetual tremor in her neatly coiffed head.

The men, sweating heavily, finally squeezed the stretcher outside, and loped off with it down to the waiting hearse. A little group of spectators stood about on the walk, morbidly staring. Inside, the people in

185

the hall began to move away as Findlay closed the two halves of the door. They murmured things to Mrs. Cooper and she said "Thank you" steadily to each one. Behind her yawned the open door of her empty rooms. With an effort, I said, "Look, perhaps I could make you a cup of tea—you don't want to be alone—"

"Come in, won't you?" she said. So I went in with her. On a round table beside the two-ring hot-plate, she set transparent cups of faded Crown Derby on an immaculate linen cloth. I couldn't think of anything to say, my tongue seemed to be asleep; but Mrs. Cooper began at once to talk, more to herself than me.

"He wanted to die, has for a long time. When I woke up and heard him, I knew what it was. And I didn't call the doctor. I just sat with him there by the bed and held his hand, and waited till it was over. He dreaded hospitals so much, he made me promise never to let him be taken there again and tormented with needles and tubes. He just wanted to die, and at home. So I waited till he wasn't breathing any more. Then I called the doctor. It was only a few hours, then he was gone. It was all I could do for him."

I looked at her with respect. She bent her head, with its immaculate white curls, to drink from the cup.

"The doctor gave me a bit of a look, but he didn't say a word. He knows us. He knew Rupert was a remarkable man. So did John Horvath. I went upstairs and asked him to come down and sit with us, before the doctor came. I wanted someone . . . someone who appreciated him . . . he looked so handsome, lying there. And John came right down, out of his sleep, though he's been drinking a lot again lately—poor John. He gave me a kiss and sat right here with me till they came and took Rupert away."

"Did he."

"And do you know what he said to me? I'll never forget it. Well, at our time of life, we know death is
186

real, not the fairy-tale we never believed in long ago. And it's such a riddle, to wonder what happens to us then. Where do we go? And Rupert was such a remarkable man, a great man really. If you don't happen to have complete Christian faith, I mean in resurrection, where does that leave you? What's there to think after a man like that dies?"

I poured her more tea.

"And do you know what John said? Sitting here beside Rupert and me, holding my hand. Our bodies, he said, they are nothing but a few cents' worth of chemicals and a quart or two of water, and yet not one atom of this is wasted after we die. So what makes you think, he said to me, that a thing so wonderful as a human soul could possibly be wasted? That makes sense, doesn't it, and it helps now. Because Rupert was such a unique man. He wrote a book on counterpoint, you know. . . . Long ago I made up my mind I'd never leave this house, we were so happy here. Rupert liked this place so much, and all our things are here, our whole lives together. . . . "

She looked around at the polished, gloomy, heavy old furniture, the fringed lamps and throng of knick-knacks. For a moment her faded eyes were bewildered, as if she did not recognize them any more; but she sat with her back as straight as an arrow and sipped more of her tea.

"My daughter will be here soon. She's flying up from Burlington."

"That's good."

"And Johnny said he would take me to the undertaker's at nine; there are things to sign, and so on—he'll take time off work; it's so good of him."

"Yes. Well, it must be getting on for nine now. I'll run along. Please let me know if there's anything I can do."

"I will, and thank you."

Downstairs again, I sat heavily, took up the book and held it. Poor woman. But I felt nothing, really.

Nothing at all. And the time moved slowly, slowly on, and the heat throbbed.

A huge thunderstorm broke over the city one day with swags of blue-green cloud lowering, a theatrical yellow light that smouldered like sulphur, and lightning cracking a white whip. When it was over and the last mutter of thunder had sulked away, the washed air smiled, sweet and clear and cool. But I was still made of lead.

"Hullo, Neil."

"Mum, you broke your promise; it's over three weeks since you called me."

"Sorry. Lost track of the time, I guess."

"You sound low. What's wrong?"

"Nothing's wrong. The heat, maybe."

"Why, it's been cool as a cave since that storm last week."

"Has it."

"Why are you low?"

"Oh, it doesn't matter. What have you been doing lately?"

"Nothing much. The house is dull and peaceful. Rosemary and the kids are up at St. Sauveur; I'll be going up this week-end."

I thought suddenly of a painting I'd seen somewhere—a crooked red house on a yellow hill with joy flying over it in the bright green sky. "That'll be nice."

"It's been worrying me not to hear from you this long time. I even went down one afternoon to that pawnbroker's Kim told me about, hung around the neighborhood a bit, hoping I might run into you."

"For God's sake, Neil, never do that. Promise you won't do that again."

"All right, if you really feel that way about it. But you do sound down, Mum. What's the trouble?"

"Oh, it's too complicated to explain. Just a bit fed up with myself, I guess."

"What have you been doing lately?"

"Oh, nothing much. Sitting under the Tree of Knowledge. The damn thing turned out to be a vegetable bore."

"—Eh?—Look, doesn't it seem crazy to you—here I am alone in town, and there you are all alone too; why the hell don't we meet somewhere for dinner? Then you'll maybe tell me what's wrong."

"No, everything's right, Neil. Everything. If I'm low it's because . . . well, because I don't seem to be the kind of person I admire. Or something. Anyway, it's a bit depressing."

"I don't follow you, dear."

"Just as well, probably. What's your idea of me, I wonder? I mean as a person, not your mum. Somebody weak and confused and illogical, I guess. A real Eve."

"The fact is, Mum, I've admired you more since you up and left than I ever did before. Once I got over my moral outrage, that is. You shook me up plenty. Ever since then I've felt different about quite a lot of things."

"What I mean is that right now . . . well, you see, I couldn't go back to your father. That kind of virtue turned out to be beyond me. But after that—"

"I see it was impossible. I mean, I saw it finally. I don't blame you. . . . Not any more. Is that what you're getting at?"

"Not exactly. But you see—well, at first I was so happy. It was such bliss to be absolutely alone. Made no sense; I mean I didn't deserve it, to be so blissful, after doing a thing like that. And now . . . "

"Well, right now you sure don't sound blissful. Why is that? What do you want you haven't got?"

"Ah, that's the point. You see, before I didn't want a single thing from a living soul. You might say I was perfectly pure. Morally spotless, I mean, no matter what I might be ethically. But somehow I got involved . . . things changed. . . . "

"Things do. But why do you feel so glum now?"

"Well, the fact is, I liked being so pure, and I don't think I'm going to be able to stand it much longer."

"Then why try?"

"Eh?"

"Why bother? Why not do what you like?"

"Son, are you giving me bad advice, at my age?"

"Why not?"

"You surprise me."

"Good. After all, it's my turn."

"I wonder if you're not right. What does it matter, really, if I can't live up to it, as long as I know what's right. . . ."

"Wait, I wish I knew what you're talking about. *Must* you be so cryptic, love?"

My knees were trembling, and my hands and lips.

"Well, dear, I'll ring off now—"

"Wait—wait—are you feeling a bit better now?"

"Not exactly. I never cared much for paprika and I hate Wilton carpets. But happiness isn't the point, you see, any more than virtue was when I left your father."

"I don't see anything, dear, except that you must be putting me on."

"Not at all. I'm being quite profound, actually. I am a damned woman. And it's something to know that much about yourself. Even more to accept it."

"Damned! How come you sound so cheerful, then?"

"Don't ask me. I'm off now, my dear. Got something to do that's irrational, so it can't wait. I'll be in touch, I really will. Have a nice week-end at the cottage."

I rang off, still trembling, and started the uphill walk home, moving fast on my rubber soles. The night shadows of the trees whispered and stirred in a light breeze. Several trillion stars looked down from heaven, their golden eyes glittering with what might well have been laughter.

Into the house I went through the front door, and straight up the stairs to Johnny's room. He was lying on the unmade bed with a drink in his hand—from the blurred look of him, the last in a long series. But the first thing he said to me was, "Jeanne Leblanc had a girl last night," with a great smile.

TRUDEAU AND OUR TIMES
Volume 1: The Magnificent Obsession
by Stephen Clarkson and Christina McCall

"Part history, part mystery, part analysis, part psychoanalysis
... Canadian writing at its best." — *Ottawa Citizen*
Winner of the Governor General's Literary Award and a
national bestseller.
0-7710-5416-5 $7.99   24 pages of b&w photos

INNOCENT CITIES
by Jack Hodgins

"One cannot but be delighted by the romping of such a fertile
imagination ... a most entertaining narrative." — *The Globe
and Mail*
"A rich, fun tale" with a cast of intriguing characters, set in
Victoria, B.C., in 1881.
0-7710-4187-X $7.99

THE BOYS OF SATURDAY NIGHT
Inside Hockey Night in Canada
by Scott Young

"A well-reported history ... a winner." — *Maclean's*
A behind-the-scenes look at Don Cherry, Ward Cornell, Dick
Irvin and the others who have made Hockey Night in Canada
this country's most successful broadcast institution.
0-7710-9097-8 $6.99   16 pages b&w photos

EVENING SNOW WILL BRING SUCH PEACE
by David Adams Richards

"A masterpiece." — *Atlantic Advocate*
A powerful, deeply affecting novel from the author of the
acclaimed *Nights Below Station Street*. Winner of the Canadian Authors Association Award for Best Fiction.
0-7710-7463-8 $5.99